TO CLAIM A SILVER CURSE

ISABELLA KHALIDI

BOOKS BY ISABELLA KHALIDI
(DARK FANTASY ROMANCE)

FORGOTTEN KINGDOM CHRONICLES
The Snows of Nissa
The Storms of Fury
The Sands of Titans
The Plains of Wrath
The Valley of Tears

STANDALONES
To Claim a Silver Curse
Buried Souls

BOOKS BY ISABELLA KHALIDI WRITING AS BELLA DURAND
(MONSTER ROMANCE)

WICKED CREATURES TALES
Roses for the Damned
Lilies for the Cursed

Don't be afraid to spread your wings and fly.

AUTHOR'S NOTE & CONTENT WARNING

PROLOGUE

Thick ebony smoke drifted towards the gloomy sky, the snake-like wisps of air dancing on the cool winter breeze. Angry flames of blazing orange and yellow raged on, swallowing up everything in their path like a vicious beast.

Screams rang out around her. Humans ran for cover, their panic stricken faces turned towards the heavens, desperate for some form of salvation.

A massive shadow of terrifying proportions slithered over the fleeing mortals. Ever so slowly, she lifted her gaze, awe and trepidation mixing in a violent concoction, threatening to consume her as she stood rooted to the spot.

A colossal snout with rows upon rows of razor sharp teeth appeared first as the rest of the creature's body came into view. Mouth gaping, her throat dried up instantly, not believing the sight before her very eyes.

Wings spanning entire fields on each side spread out as it soared over them, the silver scales of its powerful body shimmering in the dim light seeping through the dense clouds. Like a river of never-ending brilliant diamonds, it circled the burning village, its long tail whipping back and forth like a lethal flail, leveling all that stood in its vicinity.

Opening its mammoth jaw, its head tilted back as a sea of pale blue fire erupted from its center, engulfing entire blocks of buildings in its wrath, turning everything to ashes in a matter of seconds.

A cry rang out, snapping her out of her daze.

She bolted for the highest tower, the one that held the sole deliverance from the evil fiend wreaking havoc on the land and its remaining inhabitants.

Fist clenching around the iron spear, her grip unrelenting as she ran up the many steps to the dragon slaying contraption, one that every village in the entire kingdom had installed as a last desperate safety measure against the mighty beasts of legends.

It was man's only hope of ever surviving in the Land of the Kaminari, the dragons of old.

Once, many eons ago, they were ridden into battle by their distant cousins, the Raijin, lethal dragon shifters that shaped the history of the known world. Hunted down and butchered until the very last Raijin was wiped from existence, they were now only a distant memory, forever captured in the numerous heavy volumes decorating the Royal Library in the capital city of Akira.

The silver monster screeched, snapping her back to the present.

She lunged over the last few steps, sliding as a ball of fire exploded over her head. Pulling herself up, she pushed the spear into position, locking it in as she took aim.

The beast circled back, its mighty wings flapping in the wind.

She stood unmoving, counting the seconds, her hands gripping the lever as she held her breath.

Come on, come on.

As if hearing her thoughts, its head snapped around, its eyes locking on her. It roared, diving for the tower and the mortal that would bring about its eternal doom.

All sense of self-preservation abandoned her as she pulled the latch, the weapon exploding from its confinement, flying through the air at the magnificent creature charging straight at her.

It lifted its head, its powerful wings spread out wide as it opened its jaw, hovering in midair.

The spear blazed forward at the speed of light, hitting it straight on, lodging itself under the dragon's left wing, right above its monstrous heart.

Time stopped. The creature screaming into the approaching night, its pains of agony spreading across the land as it plummeted to the cold ground.

CHAPTER

1

"Two pints of beer, and make it quick."

She turned around to the gruff voice, shooting the middle-aged warrior a quick glance before pouring him his order. "A little early to be getting drunk." The clunk of glass echoed around them as she placed the drinks on the counter, her curious gaze traveling over the man's substantial form.

Rich brown curls reaching broad shoulders in cobalt blue military garments framed a stern face, the features rough yet welcoming. A ragged narrow scar cut across the male's nose, his chocolate brown eyes locked on her as she inspected him from across the bar. A neatly trimmed beard covered his square jaw, its dark shade a perfect contrast to his toffee colored lips.

A moment of silence passed between them. "I'm looking for someone." He took a sip. "Perhaps you can help me."

Squinting, she appraised him once more. A pair of gold rings shimmered on his left hand, the royal insignia of the horned phoenix like a stamp of superiority and indisputable homage to his high rank.

"What business does the Captain of the King's Guard have in this desolate village?"

The corners of his lips lifted. "Like I said, I'm looking for someone. A certain dragon slayer."

Insides clenching, she turned her back to him, pretending to be completely unaffected by the male's words as she continued to polish the row of freshly washed mugs.

"I was told he frequents this tavern. Nyro is the name that he goes by, I believe. Perhaps you've heard of him?"

"Hmm." Her mind swam. *Shit.* "What do you need a renegade dragon slayer for? I thought the Crown had their own men for taking care of unruly beasts?"

The Captain chuckled, the sound so unexpected that it got her spinning to face him. "So you *have* heard of him." A knowing look passed between them. Straightening, he threw a pair of gold coins onto the counter, his two drinks left almost completely untouched. "Tell your friend that Linus was looking for him, and that he would like to proposition him for a certain job. If he accepts, his record will be wiped clean, and he will be a free man once more. He knows where to find me."

Heart hammering away, she could only stare after the warrior as he adjusted his weapon, and without a second glance, sauntered out of the establishment.

The cloth in her hand felt heavy, her breaths coming in short, shallow gulps as she struggled to breathe, the room around her tilting on its axis. She bolted, desperate to get some oxygen into her failing lungs.

Crashing through the back door, she let the cool autumn wind sweep over her, calming her raging thoughts. As fresh air entered her shaking body, the looming panic slowly began to subside.

"Nyra?" the cook's melodic voice reached her. "What are you doing out here?"

Inhaling deep breaths, she faced the stout woman. "They found me."

A loud clang erupted around them as the clay pot in her hands came crashing down, lying in shatters around their feet. "What!? How?! What are you going to do?!"

Nyra sighed, dejected, her mind swarming with possibilities. What, indeed, was she to do? She had been on the run for so long now, hiding from the authorities and the very man that the Captain represented, always two steps ahead of them, had even come to a point when she had naively thought herself to be finally safe.

It was risky, her flighty way of life, but luckily for her, she didn't have any living family members, and so didn't have to fend for anyone but herself.

Her delusions of safety had come crashing down the moment the middle-aged warrior walked into the tavern that day, the reality that she would never be truly free laying heavy on her over-exhausted mind.

"I don't know, Margot." She palmed her face. "There's no point in running away again. If they've found me here, they'll find me anywhere."

There was only one obvious solution to her never-ending problem. Perhaps it was time that she finally accepted her fate, whatever it may be, for she was sick of living in constant fear, of thinking that at any given moment someone will come and take her away only to be locked up in some dark dungeon, never to be seen again.

"Oh, honey." The copper haired woman's arms went around her, holding Nyra close to her ample bosom. "Maybe it's for the best. This was no way to live. Besides, I'm sure they will understand once you explain everything to them."

Nyra wasn't so sure, but she really didn't have a choice, for deny it or not, her time was up.

"I'm to meet with the Captain of the King's Guard. He wants to offer me a job. Margot–" she mumbled as the cook pressed Nyra firmly onto her chest, "–you're suffocating me."

The woman released her, muttering apologies under her breath. "Seems to me like you've already made up your mind. Better to get it over with then, I suppose. Come now." A chubby arm hooked under Nyra's as they made their way to the kitchen. "The dishes aren't going to wash themselves, my dear. Best get started."

❖

The smell of ash and cedar reached Nyra Haldane as she stood in front of the temporary military barracks, the wind blowing her long red hair around her face, its vibrant hue of ripe raspberries making it appear as if her head was ablaze.

All night she had tossed and turned, her mind not allowing her even the slightest break before she finally gave up on sleeping and prepared herself. There was no point in prolonging the inevitable, she might as well get it over and done with.

So, while Margot and their guests were firmly sleeping in their warm beds, she had stolen out at the break of dawn and made her way down to the encampment.

The Captain's tent stood twenty feet from her, its ivory flaps swinging on the wind, beckoning her to step into the unknown.

You can do this, Nyra.

She remained standing.

"You know," the Captain's voice came from behind her, "it might help if you actually moved your feet. That is what walking entails."

Cursing under her breath for being caught in her moment of weakness, Nyra followed the warrior into his tent, anxious to get the formalities over with.

A large oak desk was planted at the far end of one wall, with piles of papers and a pair of brightly lit lanterns decorating its top. A makeshift bed lay a few feet away from it, covered in an array of brown furs, making it appear as if a huge bear had collapsed onto the soft mattress and was taking one of its deep slumbers on it. An adjoining room could be seen off to one side, which Nyra could only assume was a bathing chamber.

"If you're done inspecting my space," the Captain said as he moved around his desk, "perhaps we can get started. Take a seat."

"I prefer to stand."

His brows shot up, as if not used to having his orders disobeyed. "This might take a while. You would be more comfortable sitting."

"With all due respect, Captain, I didn't come here for a morning chat." She was not one to waste precious time. "If we could get this over with, I have a tavern to run."

Stroking his jaw, his eyes bore into her as she remained still, holding his intimidating gaze. "You've got quite a mouth on you. I could have you whipped for your insolence."

She smirked, the man's arrogance causing a sudden wave of irritation to wash over her. "I've faced fire-breathing dragons, it will take more than a royal uniform and a few lashes to frighten me. Besides, how did you know I was the one you were searching for?"

"I suspected, but I wasn't sure until I saw you standing in front of my tent. Now, let's see." Grabbing a paper from the closest pile, he began to read out loud, "Burglary, trespassing, fraud, assault—"

"The charges were never proven."

The Captain stood up, walking around the desk at an agonizingly slow pace, then picking up another long parchment, continued to recite, "—smuggling, theft, aiding a fugitive—" she winced "—and finally, deserting a military position." Clasping his hands behind his back, he stepped right up to her. "Scared yet?"

Anger simmered in Nyra. "If I had been allowed to leave like a normal human being then I wouldn't have been forced to do what I had to in order to survive."

"You abandoned your position."

"You gave me no fucking choice."

"Tell me, dragon slayer, do you know what the punishment is for treason?" He leaned in. "Death by a thousand cuts."

A sudden calm enveloped her, the words that were meant to scare her into compliance doing the very opposite as the not so distant memory of Nyra's last encounter with a certain winged beast wiggled into her mind.

As the fear of being scorched alive arose in her once more, making his threat of torturous execution appear childish and inconsequential.

"I have a proposition for you," the warrior continued, "one that will benefit us all, should you accept it." Moving back to his place behind the desk, the Captain plopped himself down on the awaiting chair, and opening a drawer, pulled out a palm sized object. It landed on the table's surface, the morning light shining off of it in brilliant beams of silver.

Her breath hitched.

A sly grin spread across the Captain's stern features, his eyes twinkling with victory. "She remembers." Taking the scale fragment in his hand, he twirled it, the Sun's rays reflecting off of it, blinding Nyra from where she stood. "You are to go back and finish the job that you had started all those years ago, dragon slayer. In exchange, all charges against you will be dropped, and you will be a free woman once more."

Confusion raked her insides. "I don't understand."

Chuckling, he leaned back in his chair. "You didn't kill it. The silver beast still lives."

She froze, not daring to move as his words sunk in. "Impossible," muttering, her mind raced. "I watched it plummet to the ground, my spear lodged in its chest, right above its monstrous heart."

The Captain watched her, the pads of his fingers scraping against the sharp edge of the scale. "Not quite. Raiden is an ancient dragon, one of the very first Kaminari that ever roamed the land of man. So ruthless, that no Raijin ever rode him. It will take more than an ordinary spear through the chest to kill him."

Furious for being deceived, she seethed, "Why the fuck wasn't I informed of this the first time that I was sent after him? Why make me believe that I had killed him, only to come back years later and drag me back into the whole mess again?"

Silence ensued.

The Captain's jaw ticked as he contemplated on his next words. "We weren't aware that he still lived. The village was desolate after Raiden's attack, therefore no living witnesses were present at the time to confirm his death. The previous Captain also failed to inquire about Raiden's state after your sudden departure, taking your immaculate reputation as the kingdom's best dragon slayer to be enough of a confirmation of the beast's demise. It wasn't until about a year ago that we realized how wrong we were." He sighed, palming his face. "He's burning villages left and right, not leaving a single soul alive as he goes. It appears that he's searching for something," his eyes pierced her, "a certain *someone* that had dared to threaten his life, and he won't stop until he gets his claws on her."

Realization swept over Nyra. "You mean to hand me over to him."

He cocked his head, observing her before confirming with a nod. "And to make sure that you follow through with our deal, *should* you accept it, I've added your friend's life as an added incentive. Just in case you decide to run away again, of course." He stood up, strolling over to where she stood motionless, a mask of indifference sliding into place as he inspected her. "What is one life compared to thousands, dragon slayer? If you are quick, you might just make it out alive."

They stared at each other, neither one of them daring to break the silence as Nyra slowly processed everything that had transpired ever since coming into the Captain's tent.

How the fuck did I get myself into this again?

Was this to be her destiny? To die at the mercy of some ferocious beast, the very same one whose supposed death had urged Nyra to go running from the military, abandoning her post, not being able to stomach the idea of killing another one of those magnificent creatures in cold blood?

This is madness. There has to be another way.

But what choice did she have? If she declined, they would torture her to death. If she accepted, she would most likely die in flames as the said dragon slowly roasted her body until all that remained were ashes in the wind.

Perhaps the most important question of all—was she so selfish as to knowingly sacrifice the lives of thousands of innocent people when hers could potentially save them all?

Nyra took a deep breath, her nerves settling down as she made peace with the only conclusion to her unfathomable reality. "Alright, I accept. When do I leave?"

CHAPTER

2

"This is your key," the tall, lanky woman said, placing a small, brass object into Nyra's open palm. "Second floor, last door on the left. You're lucky we had a room for you, the house will be full for the next week or so."

An elbow pressed into Nyra's back, shoving her forward onto the bar. Annoyed, she glanced back to the crowded main room, the space already overflowing with rowdy patrons.

"What's the occasion? Is it always so busy?"

Had she known it would be like this, Nyra would have chosen a different tavern for her temporary living arrangements while on her dragon slaying mission. She supposed there were other inns along the road where she might have had a more peaceful stay at, but they were much closer to Raiden's latest sighting, and she would rather not be his next fucking meal should the beast smell her in his vicinity. And dragons were known for their impossibly keen sense of smell, she wouldn't be able to escape him once he got a whiff of her.

"Tiny over there just became a father." The barmaid nodded towards a boulder of a man whose shirt was being ripped apart by a group of men, one who appeared to be already too drunk to care about the show he was putting on for his lovely guests. "He's the owner of this beauty. Seemed only fitting to have the festivities here, with his closest friends."

Arching a brow at the woman's words, Nyra ordered herself some dinner, making her way up to her room to deposit her meager belongings while she waited.

It was a cozy space, with a single bed pushed up to the far wall, the plain ivory bed setting reminding her of one of Margot's tablecloths. A small nightstand stood by its left, a sole lantern burning bright on its surface, dimly illuminating her surroundings. Aside from the olive colored armchair in the corner of the room, no other furniture decorated the space. It was common enough, and would do just fine for the duration of Nyra's stay. After all, she was a dead woman walking, and the dead had no use for material things in the afterlife. She had no choice *but* to comply with the Captain's demands, not if she wanted Margot to continue on living.

A soft knock came at her door, interrupting her train of thought. Opening it, Nyra was surprised when a pair of young girls came rushing in, carrying buckets of scalding water with them. In no time they disappeared into an adjoining room that Nyra had failed to notice upon first inspection, emptying the contents into what she assumed was the tub. Wordlessly they left her chambers, closing the door softly behind them as they went.

Not wanting the water to get cold, Nyra stripped out of her travel clothes, making haste as she washed the sweat and grime off her body. Four days had passed since she had departed from her desolate village of Minato, during which time she had barely stopped and only to relieve herself and tend to her horse before resuming once more.

She had no idea what she would do once she located Raiden, how she would even go about approaching him without giving herself away. The more she thought about it, the more she realized how insane the whole notion was.

How the hell am I supposed to kill the goddamn thing?

The first time that Nyra had come into contact with the silver beast, she had the element of surprise. Now, she was the one being hunted, by an ancient apex predator who had a target on her back.

Her stomach grumbled, pulling her back to the present. She would worry about the bloody dragon at a later date, when her insides weren't threatening to plaster themselves to each other from the lack of food.

Nyra quickly dried herself, changing into an emerald tunic and dark pants, washing the filthy garments in the cold bath water before hanging them over the side and draining the tub. Her hair was still damp as she braided it, the thick strands coming together to form an intricate design that went to the small of her back.

Satisfied with her appearance, she descended the many steps to the main room, only to find it even more packed than when she had first walked into the tavern, as if an entire village had made their new home amongst the wooden beams holding up the substantial structure, preventing it from collapsing.

Lanterns blazed in the dimly lit space, illuminating the main room, casting eerie shadows that danced on the tavern walls. Loud music tangled with the sounds of laughter and singing, the crowd over-exuberant for Nyra's dismal state.

Groaning, she planted herself firmly in front of the bar where her dinner was already laid out for her, the porridge steaming, its delicious scent of seasoned rabbit and garden vegetables causing her mouth to water. It didn't take her long to clear the plate, her insides thanking her as the last spoonful of the hot stew finally settled in her stomach.

The music grew louder, if such a thing was even possible, her ears ringing from the almost deafening noise. If only she could enjoy the festivities like everyone else seemed to be doing, but Nyra's gloomy future loomed over her like the sharp edge of a guillotine, threatening to come crashing down lest she make a single wrong move.

Sighing, her eyes wandered around the cottage style main room, taking in the many sights and sounds, pondering about Raiden and whether he was near, searching for her like she was searching for him.

That's when she felt it.

A burning sensation on the side of her face, so sudden and fierce, as if a beam of light was being directed straight at her, increasing her body temperature to impossible heights.

Frantically she searched for the source of the intrusion, for the cause of such inexplicable sensations. The shadows called to her, pulling her gaze to a single dark corner that the masses seemed to avoid, as if a plague was upon it. A giant form loomed there, hidden out of sight, watching her. Observing Nyra as she stood rooted to the spot, staring right back into the void, unable to look away.

Her skin tingled. Shivers erupted all over her body, turning into a violent wave of heat that swept over her like a raging wildfire. Her breath hitched, chest heaving from exertion, as if a force was pushing down on it, preventing her lungs from expanding.

The form from the shadows moved, straightening to its full intimidating height. A man of massive proportions stepped into the light, his gaze locked on

Nyra as he advanced, prowling like a lethal feline toward her.

Holy. Fuck.

Wide, round shoulders filled out an immaculate warrior's uniform, its front adorned with what appeared to be intricately carved scales, his broad chest tapering down to narrow hips and powerful thighs, the muscles rippling under the fabric with each sturdy step that he took, screaming with aggression.

Hair the color of shimmering moonlight cascaded down his shoulders with a few tiny braids peeking through, a portion of it swept up, revealing his devastatingly beautiful face in all its glory. His features so utterly masculine and defined, as if made to tempt by the very devil himself. Eyes of the purest sky blue bore into her, holding Nyra captive as the warrior finally came to stand a mere foot away.

Her neck craned back, his height so painfully imposing that she had the feeling of appearing miniature in his towering presence.

Her curious gaze swept over his face, drinking in the sinful sight of the giant in front of her. Light stubble covered his sharp jaw while a straight nose connected to full lips, so plump and juicy that they looked like freshly picked cherries. Her mind swirled with deliciously filthy thoughts, of what they would feel like under her tongue. Between her teeth, as she sucked them into her mouth while his massive hands roamed over her body, greedily exploring every one of her curves.

Fuck, he's gorgeous. Too gorgeous.

Unaware, she squeezed her legs, desperate to ease the pressure that was rapidly building up at the apex of her thighs.

His hand lifted, tucking a loose strand of silky hair behind her ear. She barely registered the movement as Nyra continued to stare at this stunning male specimen, absorbing his features like a parched flower would absorb water in the blazing desert Sun, her heart pounding like a hundred drums against her rib cage.

"We meet at last."

Her lids lowered at the smoky rumble, his voice vibrating with power and authority as she unconsciously nuzzled into his open palm that remained resting on her cheek, covering her entire face from how huge it was.

Leaning in, he hummed with approval, his lips grazing the shell of her ear, "Tell me your name, little vixen. Or shall I coax it out of you?" Wood and musk enveloped her, his firm body radiating with the sensual aroma, driving Nyra's desire to unbearable heights.

A breathy moan escaped her as she pulled him flush against her, his deep voice like a catalyst to the countless dirty images pouring into her mind, her nipples stiffening as heat erupted from her core. Slick flooded her panties, shamelessly dripping all over the flimsy fabric, making them utterly useless. They both froze as a desperate little whimper fluttered out of her mouth.

Bloody perfect. Why don't I just die of embarrassment, right fucking now.

Nostrils flaring, he inhaled the undeniable scent of her arousal.

"Woman," he growled, his gaze scorching, pupils dilating, the black blown so wide that only a narrow rim of blue remained. His strong arms snaked around her waist, pressing her further onto his chest, until every hard ridge of his muscled body was aligned with hers.

Callused fingers swept under her braid, digging into her scalp, tipping her head as his grip tightened.

Gods, he feels so good.

"What are you doing?" she rasped, barely holding her composure.

"Tasting you." Soft lips brushed hers, his masculine scent invading her. "Tell me to stop."

"This is crazy," she swallowed, breathless, heart hammering away as he balled her hair.

A devious grin spread across his stunning face. "Pure fucking madness." His mouth crashed down, tongue parting her lips as it dove in. Skillfully angling her head to give him better access to her hot mouth. Opening wide, she welcomed the sweet intrusion, losing herself with reckless abandon.

Fire exploded inside of her, rushing through her veins like a tidal wave, igniting her blood until all Nyra felt was the intense heat from his lips and the burning flames of desire as the massive warrior consumed her. Her clit throbbed painfully, desperate for some form of release.

Never in her life had she felt such an inexplicable pull to anyone, the all consuming need to merge with him, to be one with this devastating male so unbearable that she wanted to climb him like a tree. To entwine around him like forest vines. To make a hole in his chest and crawl so deep inside of him, that he could never be rid of her.

"What is this?" she breathed out, rattled by the speed at which everything was unfolding, then returned to feasting on his succulent lips.

"You're incredible," he muttered low, finally breaking away, a whimper escaping her as he rested his forehead on hers. "So much more than I could have ever imagined."

Confusion swept over her. "What do you mean?"

"I've been searching for you, little vixen." Her brows furrowed. "And now that I've found you, I'm never letting you go."

"I don't understand."

The devilish smirk was back again, his eyes twinkling with mischief. "You will, soon enough," then in one swift motion he hauled Nyra over his shoulder.

"What are you doing!?" Her fiery arousal was replaced with anger, hitting him frantically across his wide back. "Put me down, you animal!"

Roaring with laughter, he smacked her ass. "That I am, wildling, and the most ferocious of them all." His wide steps took them out of the tavern, Nyra thrashing on his shoulders as they disappeared into the night.

CHAPTER

3

"Where are you taking me?!" Nyra shouted, dangling down his long body. "Put me down!"

He smacked her ass again, not bothering to reply.

Her skin lit up, core gushing from his firm touch, infuriating her even more. "Will you fucking stop hitting me!?"

"No. I rather like it."

"So not only have you abducted me but you're a brute as well."

He chuckled, that deep rumble that had her rubbing her thighs together. *Damn him and his stupid self.*

"You should get used to it, wildling, you'll be staying with me from now on."

"Like hell I will!" she squealed, her fists resuming their pounding against his back. His very *solid* back. "I'm not going anywhere with you. *Put me down!*"

"You know, your squirming is only making my dick hard." She stilled instantly. "Keep it up and I'll show you just how much of a brute I really am."

Furious, she seethed, "You would force yourself on me?"

Her feet were planted on the firm ground before the last word was even out of her mouth. He leaned down, searching her gaze, silent rage staring back at her. "I may be a beast but I am no fucking rapist. I have never forced myself on a female in my entire goddamn existence, mortal, and I will certainly not start now. Besides, you will spread those pretty thighs for me soon enough. I won't even have to lift a finger as you willingly give yourself to me."

Leaning away, she swallowed, forcing her voice to be strong and unaffected as his seductive scent invaded her. "Never."

"Your mouth says one thing, but your body betrays you, little prey." He inhaled, groaning low as his fingers curled around her throat, pulling her into his personal space as he leaned in. "I can smell that sweet nectar soaking your folds, can almost taste it on my tongue every time you look at me with those big doe eyes."

"You're delusional."

"And you're aroused."

Fists clenching painfully at her sides, she attempted to tamper down the sudden urge to touch him, refusing to acknowledge her body's treachery as his lips brushed her skin.

Why the hell does he have to smell so good?

"I was thinking of my beloved," she finally managed, not backing down. *What the fuck are you talking about, Nyra? You don't have a beloved. But he doesn't know that, does he?* Grimacing at her one-sided internal dialogue, she quickly added, "Besides, you may be pretty but you're not my type."

"You don't say?" Two depthless pools of blue bore into her, his thumb playing across her thundering pulse. "Do you always kiss strangers like you want to devour them?"

Her lips parted, the not so distant memory of their heated encounter causing fresh moisture to leak out of her already drenched center.

"Deny it all you want, wildling, but sooner or later, you will be begging me to fill you up."

The arrogant prick. "You're disgusting. I would rather eat worms for the rest of my life."

A fresh wave of laughter burst from the warrior, his head thrown back with amusement. "By the gods, I may just be the luckiest male in existence." His thumb found her bottom lip, plucking at it mercilessly.

She froze, holding her breath as all kinds of wicked thoughts arose once more. Tongue itching, wanting to swipe across that thick pad of his finger that was resting just *there*, so close to her open mouth, desperate to see his reaction if she were to be brave and attempt such a blatant erotic move.

Shaking his head of silver hair in bewilderment, he pulled at her lip once more before releasing it and wordlessly resumed his walking, pulling Nyra after him as his strong fingers latched around her bicep.

"Where are you taking me?" she repeated, yanking on her arm, irritated that this infuriating man was not taking her seriously. That even now, she was imagining being naked with him, allowing him to do all kinds of dirty and depraved things to her body. "What do you plan on doing with me? And you still haven't told me your name, or shall I just call you Brute the entire time?"

Her mind swam. He should repulse her and yet—she couldn't help but wonder. What would it feel like to be the center of his attention? To be molded to his liking by his skillful hands and thick cock?

"You haven't told me yours either, little vixen." He arched a brow, his gaze heated, as if reading her filthy thoughts, shooting her a quick glance before looking away again. "But that's alright, I have *other*, more pleasurable ways of finding out." Winking, his stupid grin was back, causing all sorts of sensations to shoot through Nyra.

Don't let his pretty face fool you, he's still your captor. "You won't be touching me. The kiss was a mistake. One that will never repeat itself." She just had to remain strong.

"We'll see." He smirked, the bastard. "I do not need to touch you to have you spilling your secrets for me."

"Typical man, thinking he is a walking god amongst us mere humans."

Two narrow slits stared back at her, his features suddenly stern. "What do you know about gods, wildling? Have you ever met one?"

Nyra's thoughts flew to the ancient creature, the one that could be anywhere right now, maybe even above them while they bickered, flying on his powerful wings as he scanned the land below for any trace of her.

"Only one that haunts my dreams."

He stared at her for a long moment, as if choosing his next words, "Perhaps you haunt his dreams as well, wildling."

Perhaps, but not a day had passed that Raiden hadn't occupied Nyra's mind. Years of sleepless nights, the same scene playing over and over before her very eyes, of a magnificent silver dragon soaring straight at her while buildings burned around them. Her heartache, and the agonizing cry that had pierced through the smoke filled air as her spear lodged itself in his powerful chest. The sight of the majestic animal as it had plummeted to the ground, Nyra's heart finally shattering to pieces as that final, earthquaking crash engulfed her.

It had been the last straw for Nyra, the breaking point of her iron firm resolve. Something inside of her had snapped when the dragon's body had hit the earth. She had fled the scene in tears, without ever looking back, swearing an oath to herself that she would never again kill a dragon for as long as she lived. Her soul wouldn't be able to take it.

Yet, here you are, thinking of breaking it just to save your sorry ass.

The realization that she had been the cause of death of the mighty beasts for years on end was too much of a burden to bear, her conscience and humanity demanding she rectify her wrongs. Pay for her sins. Who was she to rid the world of such glorious beings when the gods that had created them deemed them worthy enough to exist amongst man in their mortal world?

Pathetic. Worthless. You deserve the cruelest of punishments for what you are considering doing again.

Lost in her ponderings and self-loathing, Nyra had failed to realize that her captor had released her arm and was now walking a few feet in front of her, as if not at all concerned about her potentially running away.

He thinks I'm some weak damsel. A fucking coward. Her teeth clenched. *I'll show him.*

Nyra's steps slowed, eyes darting around as she took in her surroundings. They were on some type of a narrow dirt path between two rows of trees, a forest if she had to guess, but it was too dark out, only the Full Moon illuminating the space around them, making it very hard for Nyra to distinguish what lay ahead. The fact that she had never before ventured to this part of the kingdom was an added setback to her escape plan, but no matter. She would not let it deter her.

More than ten feet separated them now, the giant warrior not once having glanced back to see where his prisoner was. Heart pounding, she took a step to the side, eyes locked on the male in front of her, then another one, preparing to launch herself into the trees at the first opportunity.

"I dare you," he said, voice low, menacing, as he slowly turned around to face her. "Give me a reason to chase you."

She regarded him, all six foot five of solid muscle and lethal calm. Massive shoulders and thighs that bulged and tensed. A fucking giant with hands that were as big as her face. Hands that had gripped her hair and held her tight to his impressive body while his mouth plundered her.

Heat rose in her once more.

For fuck's sake, get it together.

There was something so unnerving about the way he stood there, observing her. His stare focused, unblinking. Like a goddamn predator that just caught sight of his next meal, his body still, as if not breathing at all.

"I'm smaller than you." She swallowed, palms sweating from uncertainty as she backed up, fighting her instincts to stay put, to not move a fucking muscle. "Faster. You'd never catch me."

He cracked his neck, a wicked smile spreading across his full lips. "Try me."

It had to be some kind of a trick. Or maybe he just assumed his otherworldly presence would frighten her into compliance. There must have been something very wrong with her then, for no such feelings sprang forth as they faced off.

"I'm not scared of you," she said, doubting her own sanity, heart threatening to explode as the mountain of a man stared at her as if he wanted to eat her alive. And she actually enjoyed it, reveled in seeing him on the verge of tipping over because of her.

Well, shit. I might just be deranged, after all.

He closed his eyes, nostrils spreading wide, inhaling the air like some opiate addict. Or perhaps he was scenting her rising fear. Except it wasn't fear that she felt, but *excitement.* Just the thought of this powerful male chasing after her sent a new kind of rush through Nyra, one that ignited her veins and sent her core clenching with anticipation.

His lids snapped open, revealing two shimmering blue orbs, the pupils elongated black slits that froze her to the spot.

Fuck.

He cocked his head. "Run."

She bolted, rushing through the trees as her mind screamed with danger. Feet pounded against the hard ground, each step faster than the one before, chest heaving from exertion, not daring to look back lest she catch a glimpse of the man hunting her.

She must have imagined those eyes of his.

There was no fucking way that they had turned reptilian. It must have been a play of the dark, a mere trick of the shadows caused by the Full Moon—

A battering ram collided with her, sending Nyra flying forward as she toppled to the ground. Strong arms wrapped around her, fingers cupping the back of her head as if shielding her from the impact. Solid muscle pressed down as a massive body nestled between her legs, rendering her completely motionless as she lay sprawled out beneath. Panting, she became suddenly very aware of the position in which they were in.

"Little prey," smoke and velvet purred in her ear, "you shouldn't have done that. You've awoken the true beast now, and he won't rest until he's fully claimed you."

Goosebumps erupted over her skin, her nipples turning to two hard beads of stone, painful to the touch where his own chest pressed down on her. Her legs gaped open, her pussy throbbing with need as it ached to be filled up. *Traitor.*

"You can't have me." She pushed on his chest with all her might, struggling against his weight, but it was useless, as if a boulder had taken up residence in place of the stupidly handsome warrior. "Get off of me!"

"I suggest you don't do that, wildling, unless you're ready to be fucked into the dirt."

She froze.

A violent wave of arousal swept over Nyra, already imagining his fat cock slamming into her as she shamelessly begged for more. Deny it, fight it, pretend it wasn't so, but gods damn it, she would do it. She would beg him like a pathetic human being to use her, to take everything that she had to give and then some, for this was no ordinary male. Just the raw scent of him sent her blood boiling with unbridled desire.

It was savage.

Vicious.

A thrill so addictive that it left her incapable of doing anything but lie there motionless as they stared at each other, panting.

For some fucked up reason, she was immensely affected by him, and she wasn't ready to accept it. It went against all common sense and logic, everything that she had learned in her short life of twenty nine years.

"Don't fight it, little vixen." Soft lips brushed hers. "There's nothing you can do. You belong to me."

"I don't belong to anyone." She pushed at him again, refusing to give in.

Grinning wildly, he whispered against her mouth, "But you do. You just don't realize it yet."

Lips parting, she strained to take in some fresh air but too late realized her mistake. Wood and musk invaded her senses, rushing in as it filled her with the heady aroma, her body burning up as he ever so slowly licked her mouth.

A needy moan escaped her, Nyra's body betraying her, his massive erection pressing into her pulsing center as he rolled his hips over her clothes. His lush tongue dove in, gently teasing her, increasing in force until it turned into a devouring kiss, so consuming and desperate that she lost all sense of herself and the reason as to why she was running away from him in the first place. It felt right, as if she was right where she was supposed to be.

Arms locking around his neck, she pulled him flush against her, their bodies perfectly aligned, as if made for each other.

The same maddening feeling that she had back at the tavern took over, once more. The absolute need to become one with this male so unbearable, that she thought she would die on the spot.

"Tell me your name," he said, his voice unraveling the last of her resolve.

"Nyra," she whimpered, desire clouding her mind. "Please," not knowing what she was begging for, "please, I need–"

"Shh, I know what you need. But I won't fuck you here, where others can hear your screams."

Her pussy spasmed, a thick coat of cream gushing out of her, her body burning up as if hot lava was being poured over her. "I don't care, please, it's too much."

"No," he growled, eyes aflame, his face strained, as if in great pain. "The first time that I slide into your sweet cunt, it will be in my bed, where I can fuck you properly. Where you'll be laid out for me like a sacrificial lamb, so fucking desperate for my cock that I won't even have to prime you before I fill you." He yanked her hair, baring her throat to him, sucking on the flesh. "I'll stretch you so completely, you'll have no choice but to take every hard inch of me. And you *will* take every inch of me, Nyra. All of me. You'll beg me for it. Fucking *weep* for it. I am the only male that will ever give you what you need. You are *mine*. You belong to *me*."

"You're fucking insane."

Groaning, he fisted her hair, dragging his tongue up her throat and over her jaw, parting her lips to sweep in and tangle with hers, taking her breath away, yet again.

He pulled away, closing his eyes as his forehead rested on hers. "I've *been* insane, Nyra. For years, I've searched for you. Not knowing what happened to that fearless woman, if she was alive or if she had perished in that fire."

Her head pounded with confusion. Her body feverish and desperate, insides twisting, heart thundering, pussy soaking. "What fire?" she finally managed to ask, half aware of what he was saying.

A moment of silence passed as he failed to answer her, neither one of them saying anything as the air crackled between them, so thick with lust and desire that it became hard for Nyra to breathe.

She didn't know what to make of him, of his sudden changes in behavior. As if he, himself, was deeply conflicted and didn't know how to act around her, what to do with her. One minute he was angry and brooding, dragging her after him like some goddamn prisoner, and the next he was kissing her like he wanted to steal her soul for himself, like he would go mad if he didn't touch her.

She didn't understand it, this push and pull between them. Didn't dare to ponder on the true meaning of this inexplicable state that she was in.

Mere hours had passed since their meeting, and yet, regardless of her own conflicting emotions, she couldn't deny her body's reaction to him, nor the potent feeling of deeply knowing him, as if they were some long lost lovers that were reunited after many years apart.

The walls which she had erected long ago to shield herself from heartbreak seemed to be nonexistent around him, as if they had shattered at the very first glance into those oceanic eyes of his.

It was overwhelming, the intense feelings swarming her system too raw and unfiltered for her to be able to cope with them.

"I can't breathe," wheezing for air, panic threatened to consume her as her limbs began to shake.

"Nyra," her name was like a plea on his lips, full of longing and pain. "Fuck, I should have known that it would be too much for you." Lifting his giant body off, he rested on his haunches, concern coloring his features as he pulled her up into a sitting position.

"I don't understand what's happening to me."

Fingers wrapped around her throat, feeling her pulse, the motion instantly calming her, the panic dissipating as if it had never been there to begin with.

He sighed, the sound heavy with unspoken words. "It's the bond. Your human mind can't comprehend what your body is signaling."

"What the hell are you talking about?"

Cupping her face, he leaned in, surprising Nyra *yet again* when he pressed a gentle kiss to her lips. "There's no time. I must get you inside before the Sun rises once more."

"Why? What happens when the Sun rises?"

He straightened to his full intimidating height, lifting her to her feet before piercing her with a steel gaze. "The real monster comes out to play."

Before she could ask him to elaborate, he was dragging her deeper into the forest, his mask of cold indifference back in place.

CHAPTER

4

Raiden marched through the dense woods, his fingers latched around Nyra's arm, pulling the feisty redhead after him, afraid that she would run away again at the first given opportunity.

Gritting his teeth, anger bubbled up in him.

He wouldn't be able to control himself a second time around should she provoke him into a chase once more. He had barely managed to suppress the fucking urge to claim her the last time that she had done so, his inner dragon rising to the challenge, demanding he sink into her and rut her into the ground until she was well and good filled with his seed.

It was a primal instinct, one that was an integral part of all the Raijin.

And Raiden was one of the oldest of the legendary dragon shifters. One of the dozen still remaining that had yet to succumb to the curse. A dark secret so deadly that it had been kept hidden from the rest of the world for millennia.

No one knew the real truth.

Long ago, the gods had gifted a group of ruthless warriors the ability to shift into lethal beasts, to balance out their overly aggressive nature and need for violence that would ultimately lead to the demise of their mortal bodies and minds, poisoning them beyond repair. Ones that were indestructible and resilient to death, but whose ability to change back into mortal form would gradually diminish over time, until eventually they lost the ability to do so altogether, dooming them to remain in their beastly forms for all eternity. Thus becoming the Kaminari, the ferocious mythical dragons.

Unless–they found and claimed their fated mate.

Raiden was cutting it close, the curse's completion almost fully upon him, his ability now to remain in his mortal form linked to the Full Moon and its appearance in the night sky, forcing him to shift back into a dragon as soon as the Sun rose once more.

He glanced at Nyra, absorbing the heady sight of the little spitfire. She was a magnificent sight to behold, even in the current state that she was in, with her hair rumpled and clothes dirty from rolling around on the ground.

His dick jerked, remembering the feel of her warmth against him. Of the little whimpers and lustful sighs that she had made while squirming beneath him.

"You're staring," she said, facing the front.

He continued to do so, ignoring the little voice in his head telling him to throw her over his shoulder, if only to have her round ass pressed up against him once more.

"You know," she finally turned, looking straight at him, a playful glint in her big emerald eyes, "you're being awfully quiet for a man that was threatening to ravish me not too long ago."

Groaning, his head snapped back to the front, forcing the enticing memory out of his mind.

"I'm starting to think you're having second thoughts." She cocked a brow, waiting for a reaction from him. When he continued to ignore her, she continued, "You've probably realized that I'm more trouble than I'm worth. And you would be correct. I am a very complicated person, stubborn as an ass, fiercely independent—"

"Stop talking."

"—don't know how to keep my mouth shut. I can't *stand* being told what to do, and I can already tell that you're one of *those* men, the ones that crave control—"

He spun her around, hands gripping her arms like a vise. Leaning in, he muttered low, "You presume too much, wildling, and you couldn't be more wrong. I *am* a hard man. Ruthless. Demanding. A true bastard to the core." He licked her throat. "But I am also devoted, loyal, and very protective of what's mine. And you, Nyra, are *mine*."

"Stop saying that," she said, breathless. "You don't even know me."

He grinned against her neck, the urge to tell her just how well he truly did know her suffocating. To let her in on the little secret that the silver beast that she had been sent to destroy all those years ago was in fact, him.

Inhaling her sweet scent of apples and cinnamon, Raiden released her, wordlessly continuing on with their trek through the forest towards his lair.

It would probably have been an ideal time for him to let her know about the bond, and how he had recognized her for what she was to him in that burning village, when she had released that spear with the intention of killing him.

Had he not heard Nyra's voice in his mind at that very moment, urging him on to make a move, Raiden would never have suspected it, would have even burned her to the fucking ground along with everything else.

There was only one person that could talk to a Raijin through their thoughts, and the fact that after thousands of years, destiny would have it that *she* be the one sent by the Crown to put an end to the ancient dragon terrorizing the land and its people, completely unaware to what they were to each other, was still so very unfathomable to him.

Raiden glanced at her again, his gaze drawn to the little vixen like a moth to a flame, unable to help himself from basking in her presence.

My mate.

She was glorious.

A diamond in the rough.

All soft lines and delicious curves that he couldn't wait to sink his teeth into.

But it would have to wait, she didn't trust him yet, and he needed her compliant and malleable for what he had in mind. True, he could always force himself on her, take away the choice altogether, and it wasn't so uncommon for the Raijin to do so, to be rough with their females, to take without asking. But Raiden wasn't that type of male. And for some reason still unknown to him, the mere thought repulsed him.

He didn't want to just fuck Nyra.

He wanted to own her. To worship her.

To chain her fucking heart and soul to him. To render her completely useless without him. To have her addicted to him in such a profound way that she would never wish to leave him, even at his ugliest and most volatile form.

"You're staring again," she snapped at him, clearly irritated. "Just spit it out already."

His brows shot up. "I have no idea what you mean, wildling."

"Clearly, you have something to say to me, otherwise you wouldn't be looking at me like that."

"Like what?"

"Like you don't know if you want to strangle me or shove me down into the dirt."

Eyes flashing, he smirked. "Why not both?"

"Oh, for fuck's sake. Fine, will you at least tell me where we're going? I have business to attend to, you know. And as much as this little game is amusing, I *do* have somewhere to be. So if you're done playing the captor, I will be going now." She yanked on her arm, then again. When he didn't budge, she dug her heels into the ground, attempting to halt their walking.

"Nyra," he growled when she went limp, "either walk like a normal human being or I will take away your ability to do so."

"You should know by now that I'm not scared of you."

In one swift motion, he had her thrown over his shoulder, her ass jiggling in the air beside his head.

"Put me down!" she hissed, thrashing like a wild animal against him.

He smacked her ass, imagining the feel of her naked flesh beneath his palm. "I warned you, wildling. You chose not to obey me, now deal with the consequences."

"I'm not a bloody child!"

"Then stop acting like one."

Huffing and puffing and crossing her arms across her chest, Raiden couldn't help but chuckle to himself as she finally settled down. Indeed, he couldn't have asked for a more perfect female to tie himself to.

She was fierce, strong, courageous, and even more alarming, could hold her own against him, a trait that he greatly admired in her. He was a big fucker, an intimidating male. No one had ever dared to talk back to him, especially not a woman half his size.

He rubbed her thighs soothingly, needing to touch her as his mind aimlessly wandered.

At first it had started off with Raiden wanting to find his mate for selfish reasons, to stop the curse from turning him permanently into a dragon. He hadn't really cared about whether or not his mate would want him or if anything would ever come out of their bond. She would have been a means to an end, a necessary pawn in the fight for his freedom.

But something had changed that day in that village. When that tiny woman had fearlessly run against the tide, risking her own life just to save complete strangers, as if there was never a dilemma about it to begin with.

Seasoned warriors had run for the hills when faced with him. Had killed each other as an offering for an inkling of the silver beast's mercy. Yet, there she had been, a mere commoner, with no army at her back, staring Raiden dead in the eyes as she had unleashed her weapon at him. For years, those images had replayed in his head, obsessing over every little detail, driving him mad with the need to find Nyra and bind her to him.

Palm gliding along her toned muscles, he suddenly had a desperate urge to see her.

Lowering her down from his shoulders with one arm wrapped around her knees and the other cupping her head, he realized that she had actually fallen asleep.

Well, will you look at that. The wildcat likes to cuddle. Who would have guessed?

He grinned in satisfaction, inspecting her features. She looked so peaceful in his arms, the feisty woman from before replaced by this almost angelic being.

A pang hit his chest then, so sudden that it took his breath away. Unbridled rage roared through him, his blood pumping, the dragon in him clawing to get out, to destroy everything in his path that would threaten his female.

He didn't dare dissect the murderous emotions swarming his system, nor the overly disturbing fact that he would do fucking *anything* to protect this rare gem that he had just met. To make the world a safer place for the little vixen, just so that she may always sleep so peacefully in his arms.

He glanced at her lips.

Those soft, juicy lips.

Lips that he would kill for, would set the world aflame for. Lips that he had devoured not mere hours ago, that he needed to taste once more before the night was through. Lips that he could picture so vividly wrapped around his fat cock, sucking him off, draining his cum as he emptied down her tight throat.

His steps resumed, forcing the filthy thoughts out of his head, the entrance to the tunnels leading to his lair not too far away now.

For the first time in his life, Raiden didn't know what to do. How to act. He was in unchartered territory.

Never in his wildest dreams had he even imagined that the one woman that he had been searching for his entire life and the woman that had disappeared after shooting him down from the sky were the one and the same, and that he would find her once more in some desolate village tavern.

He would have laughed in any other circumstances at the absurdity of the situation. Instead, fury made Raiden see red.

She had almost killed him.

His own mate, for fuck's sake.

Would have been successful had her spear not missed its mark by a mere hairsbreadth. In any other instance, it wouldn't have made a difference, the attack on his life would have been futile, the results nonexistent, leaving Raiden unscathed and very much alive even if attempted a thousand times more.

Except, it turned out that Nyra *was* his fated mate and therefore, his only weakness. And the only way for a Raijin to die was by a blade directly to the heart administered by none other than his destined one.

Growling, he thought of all the ways that it could have gone wrong. He would have to find a way to punish his female for that little transgression.

But first—he glanced down at her, heart clenching— he would have to gain her trust. Once he had it, there would be no stopping him. He would claim her, and she would be his to do with as he pleased.

Once and for all.

CHAPTER

5

The sound of rushing water awoke her.

Blinking in the dim light, Nyra took a few moments to regain her senses as she sat up, searching her surroundings.

Domed stone ceilings with the occasional foliage hanging down from holes in a collapsed roof stretched as far and high as the eye could see, the surface rough and sharp where the stone peeked through. Stalactites with lush flora by the hundreds decorated the vast space, the pale streams of moonlight streaking in through the dolines giving the entire place an almost enchanting aura.

Stone boulders of varying sizes were scattered across the endless floor. One in particular caught Nyra's eye, its flat yet impossibly massive size reminding her of a bed. A giant's bed. Tall trees and soft grass covered the ground, giving her the undeniable feeling of being in a forest of sorts. Except, it didn't make any sense. She was in a cave.

The rushing of water reached her again, the sound so foreign in the underground chamber that she had to shake her head just to make sure her ears weren't playing a trick on her.

"You're not imagining things, wildling," the brooding warrior's smoky voice came from behind her. "That's a waterfall that you're hearing."

Stunned, she turned to look up at him. "But how is that possible? We're underground."

Crouching down in front of her, he studied her with his piercing blue gaze. "Yes, deep in the belly of the Kruka Mountains."

"What?!" her mouth gaped open. "That's days worth of walking! How long have been I asleep? How the hell did we get here?"

"Not long," pause, "I carried you."

Laughter exploded around them. "You must think I'm bloody stupid."

"I'd prefer to call it very close-minded."

She scoffed. "You're an ass, you know that?"

"Yes, but a very handsome one." His pearly whites made an appearance, eyes glinting with amusement.

"And annoying as fuck."

His grin widened, tempting Nyra to smack it right off his beautiful face. "That's not a word I'd use to describe my fucking."

"How humble of you. I'm sure the ladies throw themselves off a cliff once you're done with them."

A chuckle, and then, "I had to save quite a number of them, actually. You can't imagine the lengths some women would go just to remain in my bed."

She rolled her eyes. *But of course.* "I'm sure that's just so that they can set it on fire, since they can't exactly wipe the memory of your giant naked body from their brain."

He bit his lower lip, as if restraining a laugh. "I'm very unforgettable, wildling."

"And very arrogant, it would seem."

"You love it."

"I prefer men whose heads aren't on the verge of exploding."

He smirked, the bastard. "No one's ever complained about the size of my head before."

Ignoring the obvious innuendo, she said, "Clearly, there's something very wrong with them."

"Yes, they're not you."

Speechless, Nyra could only stare at the massive male still crouched in front of her, dead serious, eyes scorching, as if all the humor had left him with that last admission and had been replaced with something much more dangerous.

Her heart skipped, the air around them sizzling. "You're giving me a goddamn headache with all of your changing moods. It's very confusing, I can't keep up with you."

"Then let me make it clearer, pretty girl." His hand reached out, his knuckles grazing her cheek. "What is it that confuses you?"

"Everything." She swallowed, blood pounding in her ears. "For starters, you still haven't told me your name. You went from kissing me like you were starving to almost running me over like a rabid bull. Then in the span of mere moments, you called me an idiot and something akin to a rarity. I have no idea what you want from me, why I'm even here in the first place or how long you plan on keeping me."

Callused fingers wrapped around the back of her neck, his thumb stroking her thundering pulse. Days seemed to pass as they stared at each other, Nyra's heart thrashing in her rib cage, her skin on the verge of melting from his heated gaze.

"I already told you what I want from you, wildling. Nothing's changed," his voice dropped, eyes lowering to her mouth, sending a shiver down her spine. "There is much that you don't understand, Nyra. Much that you still have to learn. That does not mean that you are stupid, nor did I ever imply such a thing."

Her voice shook, breathless, "You said I was close-minded."

"I did," his lips brushed her jaw, lightly pecking it as he spoke, "and I stand by what I said. You are not aware of anything other than the world which you have been shown by the people around you. You live in an illusion, a half-truth, completely unaware of the reality of the universe." His eyes softened, cupping her face with both palms as he lowered himself onto his knees, spreading them so she was nestled in between. "But–the fault doesn't lie with you. I will teach you, Nyra. I will be your anchor. Your guiding light. All I ask is that you trust me. I would never do anything to hurt you."

"You stole me away."

"I did, and I won't apologize for that."

Furious, she wrapped her fingers around his wrists, attempting to push him away. "You do realize how absurd you sound. You're asking me to put my faith in you—a complete stranger. *My fucking captor.* A man that I met hours ago, that's holding me against my will."

"Have I harmed you?" A hand slipped into her hair, gripping it, the other hand wrapping around her throat, his voice so low she could feel the vibrations across her skin.

"No," she rasped.

"Have I done anything to make you feel threatened?"

Shivers erupted over her, his nose trailing a path down her neck and over her collarbones, her voice breathless as she attempted to form an answer, "No, but you're unreliable and I have no idea what to expect, if you're going to crush me or hurl me across the air."

Fisting her hair, her head tipped back, her neck laid open to him in silent offering as his nose trailed over it. "Make no mistake, wildling, I will do all kinds of wicked things to you. Things you can't even begin to wrap your pretty little head around. Things that will make you question your sanity and willingness to offer yourself up to me on a silver platter," he murmured by her ear as his other arm wound around her, crushing her body to him.

She shuddered, his warm breath heating her skin as he inhaled deep.

"You smell like heaven and sin. Like the winds on a cool summer breeze, so fucking tempting that I'm going crazy with the need to claim you."

He shot up, lifting her along so that her legs wrapped around his waist. Two large hands grabbed her ass, squeezing it roughly as he carried her off.

"What are you doing?" She hung on to his thick neck, her pussy clenching, panties already drenched. "Where are you taking me?"

Oh, gods, I think I might faint.

Two blue orbs seared into Nyra, as if sensing her panic, as if able to see right through to her very soul, his voice dripping with danger as he rumbled, "Don't worry, little vixen, I'm not going to fuck you. Not yet, anyway."

Don't you dare be disappointed. Look at the size of him, he'd rip you apart.

He squeezed her ass again, tucking his face into the crook of her neck as he ground her against his massive erection, inhaling her scent.

She bit her lip, holding back the humiliatingly loud moan. *Fucking hell. He's huge.* Her clit throbbed, endless sparks shooting across her wired body.

"Sweet little prey, how I ache for you."

Breathe, Nyra.

He inhaled again, then dragged his tongue up the side of her neck, her face, her lips. "Give me your mouth, woman."

Begrudgingly, she shook her head, turning away from him, if only to give herself a break from the intense wave of energy rolling off of him, naively thinking that she would be able to keep true to her promise of never kissing this infuriatingly alluring male ever again.

Something akin to a snarl met her refusal, like the sound a deadly predator makes before attacking his next victim. He yanked her hair, hard, slight pain shooting through her as he dove for her lips again. "Give. Me. Your fucking. Mouth."

"Make me," she challenged, her mind and body conflicted, on the verge of shutting down from the heat of his body and the intensity of his gaze.

He growled, shoving her hard onto his erection, "You *will* obey me, wildling," then crushed his lips to hers before throwing her into a pool of water.

Waves of warmth washed over Nyra as her head plunged below the surface, enveloping her in a soothing embrace. For a brief moment in time, she forgot where she was, the sensation so sublime, her tired muscles weeping with joy. Her lungs protested, pleading with her to take in much needed oxygen.

Her head burst from the surface, only to see the mountain of a warrior staring down at her, a big smirk on his stupidly smug face.

"I swear to you," she hissed, glaring at him, her chin still lowered in the water, "I will break your fucking limbs if you come anywhere near me right now."

His smirk widened, eyes glinting with mischief. "Don't tempt me, little vixen. Violence makes my dick hard."

Of course it does, sadistic maniac.

He cocked his head, a wide smile spreading across his handsome features, causing Nyra's breath to catch as she wordlessly stared back at him. It was blinding, the smile like a knife to her chest, so painfully beautiful that she cursed the heavens for her bad luck.

Of all the times that she could have met such a rare specimen of the male population, it had to be now, while she was hunting for a beast that would kill her the very instant it sighted her, thus ending any possibilities for this attraction that was brewing between them blossoming into something more substantial.

She winced, taken aback by her train of thought. *What the hell are you thinking? He's an arrogant, condescending barbarian and most likely whores himself all over the kingdom. You'd be just another notch on his bedpost.*

"No, Nyra, you'd be the last one."

Sure that she had said her thoughts out loud, she watched his face fall, all the humor gone, replaced once again by his usual glowering demeanor.

"Wash up, I'm going to prepare you some food. And then, I'll tell you a story."

Before she could protest, he was already walking away, only his imposing shadow now visible as he stalked out of sight.

CHAPTER

6

Beads of water trickled down her naked flesh, her muscles loosening as Nyra continued to wash herself.

She had debated bathing fully clothed but then realized how absolutely ridiculous it would be. Had the menacing warrior wanted to take advantage of her he could have done so a countless number of times already. He could easily hold her down with one hand. They had been alone for half the night and there would have been no one to stop the giant of a man from having his way with her had he wished it so.

As much as he was the savage that she recognized him to be, he could also be surprisingly gentle. A hint of some deep rooted pain lay hidden in those magnificent blue eyes of his, a longing that seemed to appear in a flash when he stared deep into her eyes before vanishing once more, making Nyra question whether it had been there to begin with.

The voice of reason in her head seemed to be severely conflicted. It was more than obvious that she should have been using this time while alone and unguarded to find a way to escape instead of having a leisurely bath, but for some fucked up reason she couldn't bring herself to care.

Where would she go, anyway?

There was no one waiting for her. No one that would wonder where she had gone. Sure, Margot might think of her once in a while, but Nyra had already said her final goodbyes to the cook, making peace with the high possibility that she would die in this dragon slaying mission one way or another and hence never see Margot again. And the Captain—well, he would most likely assume that the beast had eaten her once she failed to return in one piece.

There was also the undeniable pull between Nyra and her captor that she couldn't ignore. If she were to die soon, she might as well indulge in her carnal urges, and who better with than that brooding chunk of raw masculinity.

With those thoughts in mind, Nyra had stripped out of her clothing, laying them out to dry on some rock on the side, and got to cleaning herself.

It felt good to wash the dirt and grass stains off her flesh, to allow the warm water to cleanse away the slight apprehension that she had felt ever since leaving the tavern. Which was another confabulation in itself, that instead of fear and trepidation, Nyra felt alarmingly safe and protected in her captor's presence, as if the gloomy male had instilled a sense of calm in her, never once doubting his intentions and sincerity to never harm her.

"He made his intentions clear, alright," she muttered to herself, wringing her hair, replaying every moment since their encounter in the inn.

"Did I, now?"

She spun around.

Her breath hitched.

Ah, shit.

Her smug captor was standing at the edge of the pool, shirtless, his chiseled torso on full display. Wide shoulders bursting with strength and a chest and abdomen so perfectly sculpted that rows upon rows of muscles that Nyra hadn't even been aware existed were immaculately etched into his giant warrior's body. If she had thought him beautiful before, there were no words to describe the virile man standing before her, oozing with raw sexual power.

As if reading her mind, he smirked, unbuttoning his pants, his eyes locked on her.

"What the hell are you doing?" she breathed, her voice faltering, her own nakedness completely forgotten about as his pants dropped.

"Taking a bath."

Nyra's mind went blank. Her mouth hanging open, saliva collecting at the corners as she took him in.

Of course he has to look like a fucking god.

Massive thighs that could crush a man's skull held up his impressive body, his calves elongated but equally defined. Her head tilted, her gaze sliding to his groin, where a monster of a cock hung heavy; long, thick, with bulging veins running over velvety steel, just begging to be traced with her tongue. She greedily licked her lips, imagining the feel of it.

"You're drooling."

Her nipples pebbled, skin erupting in goose bumps, his husky voice only adding to the heady temptation that was all him, her arousal spiking to concerning levels.

Unable to look away, Nyra watched as he lowered himself into the pool, the surface rippling around his rugged body as he stalked towards her.

She backed up, transfixed, still too lost in whatever the hell was happening at the moment to care about her exposed breasts and her stiff nipples pointing straight at him as if beckoning him, aching to be touched.

"I'm not, I've seen better," she said, her voice lower than she'd like, feigning indifference when her insides were doing somersaults, her body on the verge of combusting.

The cool stone hit her back, halting her further movements.

She gasped.

"What's the matter, wildling?" Amusement and something sinister radiated off of him as he advanced on her. "Not so brave anymore." His eyes were half-lidded as his gaze swept over Nyra, branding her like a physical caress.

Her skin burned. Heart pounding, chest heaving as he came within an inch of her, so close she could smell his woodsy scent, could feel the heat rolling off of him in waves. Could see the raw hunger in his eyes and the delicate thread of control that he was barely holding on to.

A droplet of water trickled down her face, her neck, her collarbones, his intense gaze following it as it trailed down her flesh, resting finally on her pert nipple. His eyes darkened, flashing with danger, causing the tight bud to stiffen even more. Moisture leaking out of her core, pussy clenching, begging to be filled up.

Her lids dropped, head craning back as she stared at him, mesmerized by the glorious male in front of her.

His hand lifted.

She whimpered, internally pleading for him to touch her, to put her out of her fucking misery already. To ease the devastating pressure that was rapidly rising in her.

"You're trembling." His hand halted, brows knitting together as he searched her face. "I'm not going to hurt you."

Shaking her head, no words came forth to dissuade him, to convince him of the false notion that she was afraid of him, that the reason for her trembling was not fear but an overwhelming sense of unadulterated desire. Nyra could only stare, hypnotized, as he slowly backed up and leaned on the opposite side of the pool's edge, arms spread out, braced on the stone wall behind him.

Disappointment and confusion raked her insides, his abrupt withdrawal and lack of action contradictory to his possessive nature that Nyra realized was like an aphrodisiac to her.

Maybe he's not as attracted to you as you are to him.

Swallowing down the bitter lump of rejection and clearing her throat, she lowered herself into the water until her shoulders sank underneath. "I thought you were going to make us some food."

His head tipped back, resting on the stone as his eyes drifted shut. "Is that really what's bothering you, wildling?" Her brows furrowed. "Ask me what you really want to know."

"I–uh–" she shook her head, not understanding his words. Not understanding the suddenly angry scowl marking his striking features as his lids lifted. Nor the heady way that he was staring at her, as if at war with himself, as if suffering, silently begging Nyra, but for what, she wasn't sure.

"What happened to that fearless woman," he said, his tone cold, dripping with venom, "the one that had dared to defy me in the forest, giving me the chase of my life?" He cocked his head. "The one that had shot down a fucking dragon from the sky, completely ignorant of the fire raging on around her?"

Her breath caught. "How do you know about that?"

Blue flames danced in his eyes, challenging her. "I know a lot of things, wildling. It's you that baffles me. Now," he leaned forward, eyes blazing, "*ask me.*"

Heart pounding, she studied him, alarm bells going off somewhere in the back of her mind, questioning herself and what her intuition was telling her, choosing to take the easier route. "Tell me your name."

"Coward," he spat, his muscular arms stretched out, his wide chest on full display. "Try again."

"I. Want. To. Know. Your. Name."

"Ask me what you *really* want to know, Nyra," he growled, the water around him bubbling, "and if you're honest, I will tell you my fucking name."

The nerve of him.

Chest heaving, she glided forward, one step at a time, then another one, and again, keeping herself hidden under the water, her eyes never straying from the warrior, until barely an arms length separated their naked bodies.

I'm going to die anyway. No reason to feint modesty.

Her pulse raced. Heart palpitating, skin tingling from the ferocity of his stare.

I'm no coward, damn him and his stupid self.

He grinned triumphantly. "Say. It."

She straightened, tiny beads of water rushing down her naked flesh as Nyra emerged from the pool, her body dripping wet right in front of him.

"Your name," she hissed. "What is it?"

His arm shot out, pulling her onto his lap until she straddled him. "Wrong fucking question. Ask me," he murmured by her ear, fingers digging into her hips as he ground her down over his erection, "why I didn't touch you. Why I didn't dip my fingers into your pretty little pussy and make you cum all over me."

"Fuck you," she half-seethed through a moan, pushing at his chest, her body shaking all over once more his vicinity, from the surge of heat in her throbbing core.

"*Ask me,*" he growled, yanking her head back by the hair, his big cock settling in the crease of her ass, "how

I've kept my fucking hands off you when all I've been able to think about is spreading you and feasting on your dripping pink cunt."

"Who said I'd let you?" A full body shiver swept over her as his nose trailed up her throat. Her nipples ached, brushing against his bare chest.

He pulled her hair, pushing her breast out as her back arched. "Oh, you'd let me, wildling." His tongue swirled around one hard bud, then the other, tasting her. "You'd beg me so prettily," – *lick* – "so eagerly," – *lick* – "so willingly," *lick, lick* –

"You smug bas–" she cried out, his hot mouth clamping down on her nipple. Biting, sucking, teasing it as if it was his favorite meal. As if trying to see just how viciously he could suck the tight peak into his greedy mouth before she completely lost her damn mind and truly begged him to ruin her.

"You were saying?" he chuckled before biting down again.

Fingers dug into his shoulders as Nyra clawed at him, his hold unforgiving. Slight pain shooting through her as he mercilessly fisted her hair, the other hand rolling and pinching her other nipple, shudders overtaking her.

Unknowingly, she began to rock her hips, grinding against his thick cock, the smooth shaft rubbing her swollen clit.

"*There she is*," he growled, squeezing her ass with both hands, "my fierce little vixen, taking what she needs from me."

She was so obscenely wet. So utterly and undeniably drenched, that Nyra thanked the heavens for the small mercy of being in a pool of water, where the arrogant male wouldn't be able to discern just how soaked she truly was. Where she could pretend that the slick pouring out of her aching center wasn't her body's treachery and raw desire for him. Where she could fight the confusing emotions battling inside of her. Otherwise, Nyra was sure she would never hear the end of his insufferable gloating. Nor would she be able to pretend that she hated him anymore.

"Hmm," he hummed against her nipple before sucking hard, "fucking delicious," spreading her ass then ruthlessly squeezing it together, a snug pocket forming around his steel shaft. "And to think I almost lost this."

"What are you talking about?" A loud, embarrassingly wanton wail burst from her as his swollen head rubbed against her entrance. Her pussy contracting around it, as if trying to suck in the bulbous crown.

A loud pop sounded as he released her flesh. "Bloody hell, woman," he groaned, teeth clenching, "your greedy little cunt is desperate for my fat cock, isn't she?"

Nyra shook her head vigorously, bolting her mouth shut before another moan could escape, refusing to give him the satisfaction of knowing just how much she craved him.

All of him.

"I bet she's gaping wide open for me."

"Like I said," breathless, false bravado speaking from her, "you're delusional."

In one swift motion, she found herself being spun around and lifted out of the water, her ass planted on the edge of the shimmering pool.

Her captor pushed on her chest, pressing her down onto the ground, his massive hands gliding down her slick body, palming her curves before hooking both arms under her thighs and pulling her forward.

"I wonder," he whispered, her skin burning under his touch as his eyes zeroed in on the apex of her thighs, "what will I find when I open these legs?" Licking his full lips, his heavy cock jerked in midair.

A treasonous whimper met him, Nyra's fists clenching at her sides. "I'm dry as the fucking desert. Might as well give up."

Growling, he pushed her knees all the way back, revealing her soaked pussy to him. A deep flush coated her body as he leaned in, inspecting her with lethal focus. Shame for being so completely exposed overtook her, for the indisputable proof of her arousal that was dripping down her ass.

His fingers brushed against her, dipping into her cream before lifting them up for Nyra to see.

Oh, shit.

"Tha–that's water."

He smirked, reverently sucking his fingers clean, his pupils blown wide as he groaned. "There you go lying again, wildling. I think it's time I finally taught you a lesson."

Precum leaked from his swollen crown, dripping onto her lower stomach. The sudden urge to rub it into her skin took over. She bit her lip, contemplating if it would be too soon to show him the hidden depraved side of herself.

"Do it."

Her eyes shot up. They stared at each other in silence, only their heavy breathing and the pounding of their hearts echoing around them, as if nothing and no one else existed in the world but the two of them and this very moment that seemed to stretch on forever.

"*Do. It.*"

"Tell me your name."

He snarled, actually fucking snarled at her, eyes ablaze, his hands still pressing her knees back, his long silver hair shimmering as he hovered above her like a merciless god of thunder.

"Tell me," she breathed, eyes locked on him, her fingers slowly gliding through his juices. "Please."

Something vicious snapped in him, as if a switch had gone off, as if her words triggered the delicate hold on his control, turning him into a murderous beast.

Bending over, he licked a path up her body through his arousal, spreading it everywhere as his tongue swirled in every dip and hollow, around her tight nipples, biting them. Up, up, and in between her collarbones, the column of her throat, nipping the skin, sucking her earlobe before his tongue lashed out again, pulling moans out of Nyra as his giant body nestled in between her thighs.

One massive hand wrapped around her throat, the other circling her drenched entrance.

"My *name...*" he murmured into her ear, smirking. "Well, you'll find out soon enough." His fingers plunged in. "Now, start your fucking screaming, wildling," and for the first time in her life, Nyra obeyed

CHAPTER

7

His cock throbbed. Jerking against the little vixen, Raiden's digits pumping languidly inside of her as he sucked on Nyra's tight nipples.

He didn't know how long he would be able to hold back, but he knew that he had to. For both of their sakes. It was one thing to fuck around with nameless women, ones that had never been more than a much needed physical release for Raiden, and it was another whole world when his fated mate was concerned.

It was imperative that Nyra knew what she was getting herself into before she fully gave her body to him. To be acquainted with both the good and the ugly side of him. He wouldn't have it any other way, no matter how his blood boiled with unbridled desire for her. No matter how badly his dick ached and pleaded with him to sink into her intoxicating warmth. Nor how desperately the dragon in him thrashed to come to the surface and lay a claim on her so that no other male would ever even dream about attempting anything with the infuriatingly defiant female.

Her moans of pleasure were pure fucking torture as his digits curled and scissored inside of her. As she grabbed a handful of his hair while he feasted on her succulent buds, gyrating against him like the greedy little wildcat that she was.

"Oh, fuck," she croaked, her pussy gushing around him. "Oh fuck, oh gods."

A medal of honor should be awaiting for him somewhere in the heavens for the control that he was still barely holding on to as the heady scent of her arousal reached his nostrils, infiltrating every gods forsaken atom of his being, turning him feral when her desperate mewls and soft whimpers filled his ears. When she moaned for him, as if he was the only one that would ever be able to give her what she needed.

Which he was.

Tonight he would show her his generous side. His soft side. *Tomorrow*...a sly smirk spread across his face. Tomorrow, she would meet his volatile one. The one that she must learn to accept without reservations for their bond to be fruitful. For the both of them.

A sudden urge to taste her overtook Raiden. Open mouthed kisses trailed down her soft body, his tongue and lips savoring her flesh as he made his way down to his grand prize.

Sounds of protest met him as he slipped his fingers free of her tight canal, only to be replaced with a breathless moan and a sharp sting to his scalp as Raiden dragged his tongue from her back hole to her clit, over and over again. Sucking in the swollen nub before drawing slow, torturous circles around it. His hands gripped her thighs, keeping them nice and spread for him as he ate her out.

Raiden could spend the rest of his existence between her legs, lapping up her sweet honey. Drinking from her pretty pussy as if it was a golden well.

"It's too much," Nyra rasped, yanking hard on his hair as she squirmed beneath him. "Please."

Rumbling with satisfaction, he pressed three digits back into her, imagining it to be his fat cock that her tight little cunt was squeezing the very life out of. That it was his rock hard shaft that was rubbing her inner walls, coating it with her cream as she began to clamp up.

"There you go," he groaned, watching her. "Just. Like. *That.*" Then flicked her clit one last time as she exploded, convulsing under him as he held her down.

A fresh load of warm milk drizzled out of his swollen crown, his dick weeping like a virginal boy for his delectable mate into the pool below.

What a waste. His gaze shot to Nyra, pride swelling in his chest when he saw the satisfied look on her beautiful face. *Soon,* he grinned, his balls tightening in anticipation, *she'll make up for this. I'll make sure she's taken every last drop of me direct from the source.*

He swiped her sensitive little nub one last time then sucked his fingers dry once her tremors subsided, relishing in the fact that he had been the one to drive the feisty female over the edge. Crawling over her, he crushed his lips to hers before she could protest.

Their tongues tangled, mouths molding together as Raiden deepened the kiss. Nyra's legs wrapped around him, holding him like a vise, pressing Raiden's engorged crown dangerously close to her entrance.

"Careful," he warned, licking the inside of her mouth, "even I have my limits, wildling," then her jaw and throat. Fists full of her round breasts, he sucked on both nipples before releasing them with a wet pop, kissing a trail down to her mound before climbing off of her.

"Wait–"

"Get dressed, Nyra." He turned around, stalking to the other end of the pool where his garments lay in a pile. Needing to get away from her as fast as possible before he did something that she would regret later.

He quickly dressed himself, his back turned to the little vixen, giving both of them time to regain their composure. Choosing to ignore his still throbbing dick that was refusing to deflate.

"There are some fresh clothes over there on the rock." He pointed to somewhere behind him, avoiding the odd aching sensation in his chest.

She'll thank me later, when arousal isn't clouding her mind.

Soft rustling filled his ears as Nyra wordlessly dressed herself, avoiding to acknowledge the tense silence surrounding them.

"I've brought you something to eat," he popped the buttons of his pants in place, moving swiftly to a smaller flat boulder where a tray filled with food awaited. "Come, sit." Lowering onto the ground, he patted at a spot beside him.

"I'm not a dog."

Raiden's gaze shot up. Dark pools of green stared back at him, blazing with barely contained rage that was mirrored in the fury emanating from Nyra. "I'm aware."

"Are you?" she crossed her arms, glaring daggers at him. "Because you've done nothing but lead me around by a tight leash, play with me for your own amusement, and as of right now, attempt to pacify me by feeding me, most likely from the palm of your hand by the way you're holding that piece of fruit."

He glanced down, clenching his teeth in annoyance when he realized how his genuine gesture might appear degrading to others. "You're angry with me."

"That would imply I care. I don't."

He grabbed her wrist, pulling her down onto his lap. "I thought we had already established that you're a lousy liar, wildcat." Shivers erupted over her skin as

Raiden murmured by her ear, a sense of deep contentment rolling through him when she lightly trembled against him. "It seems that I've left you unsatisfied. Perhaps fruit is not what you crave. Perhaps, you're hungry for something else, something that has been denied to you."

"I don't know what you're talking about." Her chin lifted, arms locked together over her chest, avoiding his stare.

He chuckled, Nyra's meek attempts at acting cool and collected only adding fuel to his urge to tease. "Yes, you do, and I promise you, we'll have all the time in the world for me to get acquainted with your delectable body." Her skin flushed, a piece of fruit hovering by her mouth, nudging her lips as he spoke, "You need to eat, pretty girl. You haven't eaten anything since the tavern and I'd rather not have you passed out from starvation. Besides, I can't fuck you properly if you're weak."

A beat of silence, and then, "Oh."

"Open."

She did so, Raiden's heart swelling when she obliged, the tender slice of mango sliding into her mouth as he started to hand feed her, his other arm locked around her waist.

Juices dripped down the corner of her mouth, tempting him. Threading his fingers into her hair and tipping her head slightly, he licked the sweetness off Nyra's face. Groaning as the fresh scent of her arousal reached him, his dick swelling in his pants against her thigh.

Fuck. This is torture. Just get on with it already, before the Sun comes up and she loses her shit.

He palmed his face, debating on how to broach the entire subject of fated mates and the curse of the Raijin. Where to begin so that she doesn't think him crazy, or worse, scare her away.

"Nyra," he said, drawing lazy circles on her arm, "I need to tell you something."

Her gaze narrowed, slowly chewing on the piece fruit as she started to move away, Raiden's heavy suspicions of Nyra being hurt too many times for her to be able to trust anyone being confirmed by that singular action.

He grabbed her, pressing her close. "No running, I thought I already told you that your place is by my side. Now, I wish to tell you a story. Be a good girl and keep an open mind. You can ask me anything, but only once you've had your fill."

Mouth full of food, she protested, "This is too much. There's enough to feed three people–"

He shoved another slice of mango into her mouth, silencing her protests. "Seems like you've got room for some more in there."

If looks could kill, Raiden would be a dead male already. But he didn't really have a choice, he was running out of time. She had to know who and what he was, and what she meant to him. But first–

"How did you become a dragon slayer?"

Bits of mango flew out of Nyra's mouth, coughing and spluttering as she tried to catch her breath.

"What–" she cleared her throat, "What makes you think I'm a dragon slayer?"

He searched her face, gaze bouncing between her big eyes. *This is it. No turning back now.* "I was there that day," he said, "when you shot down the silver dragon. I saw you."

Mouth hanging wide open, she didn't reply. Her face pale, as if all the life had been drained from it.

He cocked his head. "Is everything alright?"

"I–" she tried to move again, but Raiden's hand held her firmly in place. "I don't want to talk about it."

"Why not?"

"Because it's not a part of my life that I wish to remember."

Interesting. "If I didn't know any better, I'd say you're hiding something. What is it, wildling?"

Lowering her head, her voice was almost a whisper as she admitted, "I was a different person back then. I did things that I'm not proud of. Things that haunt me to this day."

If only she would open her mind and let him in. But it was bolted shut, as if tower-high walls had been erected inside of it.

"Tell me."

Shaking her head, Nyra turned away from Raiden. He grabbed her chin, forcing her to face him once more, frustration and anger bubbling up inside of him. Frustration with himself for the poor job that he had done in gaining her trust, and anger with the pieces of shit that had made her feel so dejected and worthless.

"Don't you dare hide from me, Nyra. I'm not like those pathetic little humans that you've had the displeasure of knowing your entire life. I will never judge you. Whatever it is that you keep locked away in your heart, you can trust me to keep it safe." He leaned in, kissing her softly, stroking her hair as tears welled up in her eyes. "I will never hurt you."

"I don't know what's wrong with me," she whispered, gazing at him. A single tear made its way down her cheek, Raiden's thumb capturing it. "I never cry. But when I'm with you..." she trailed off, eyes wide. "I feel like you understand me. I find myself wanting to tell you my secrets, as if deep down, I know that you won't abuse them. And even though we've only met last night, I feel as if I've known you my entire life."

He tucked a strand of hair behind her ear. "That's because your soul recognizes me, little prey."

"What do you mean?"

"Tell me first what it is that haunts you."

Silence stretched between them before Nyra finally opened her mouth. "I'm ashamed," she admitted, voice breaking, "Of myself. Of the lives I've taken as a dragon slayer. Some might say that I was doing the kingdom a service, that I was tolling out justice against the ruthless creatures terrorizing the land. That it was required when so many innocent people couldn't defend themselves."

"But you don't feel this way?"

"No," she shook her head, wiping her moist eyes, "not anymore. I used to believe that I was doing the right thing. That being a dragon slayer was humane, that it was a necessary evil against such ferocious beasts. How could a mere human defend himself from such an animal? It is almost impossible. And so, I took it upon myself, believing that there was no other way." He stroked her back, languidly tracing the slope of her spine. "There were times when I had my doubts, when reports that I was given by the Captain of the King's Guard didn't make much sense, but I ignored them, taking his word, trusting him to speak the truth. But then, on the last mission, something changed. It was as if something had broken in me."

Raiden listened to her, not wanting to interrupt the precious moment where she was finally opening up to him. He felt it in his bones that it was something that he needed to guard at all costs.

"You should have seen him," she said, gaze somewhere off, far away, as if reliving a long lost memory, awe replacing her sorrow stricken features. "He was magnificent. The biggest dragon that I have ever seen. Pure silver, with massive wings and flames so bright that it could blind a man." She glanced at Raiden, inspecting him. "His eyes were so blue it was as if the sky was captured in them. As if he could see right through to my very soul." A flicker of something flashed in her eyes, there and gone before Raiden could latch on to it. "Much like yours, actually," she muttered, so low he almost missed it.

My bright little mate. "What happened to him?"

Silence, and then, "I thought I killed him." Tears streamed down Nyra's face as she stared at Raiden, never once breaking eye contact with him as they drenched her face. "But then I discovered that he had survived, and that I am to go back and finish the job that I was entrusted to do the first time. I must kill the beast to be pardoned for abandoning my military position, otherwise I'll die."

Raiden sucked in a strained breath. Would she betray him?

"The thing is," she turned fully towards him, straddling his thighs, "I can't do it, not even to save my own life. I don't want to be the reason that beautiful creature never roams the world again."

A sigh of relief escaped him, her willingness to sacrifice herself for him easing his fears, before awareness struck him.

"I'll burn them all to the fucking ground before I let anyone touch you, Nyra. You're mine, and I protect what's mine."

Sorrow and pain laced her features. "What is one man compared to an entire army?"

A satisfied smirk made its appearance on his face, relishing in the moment of Nyra's complete ignorance before all hell broke loose.

"That may be true, wildling, had I been an ordinary male." He leaned in, inhaling her apple and cinnamon scent. "As luck would have it, I'm a Raijin. And *you*," his arms wound around her, "are my fated mate."

CHAPTER

8

Loud laughter echoed around them, Nyra's head thrown back with amusement before she suddenly schooled her features. "Unbelievable. Just how stupid do you think I really am?"

"What? Nyra–"

She frowned, pushing on his chest. "Please let me go, I wish to stand."

He pulled her back. "No."

"Yes," shoving at him, fury making her see red as the infuriating male tightened his hold.

"Don't fight me. I'm not letting you go."

Clenching her teeth, she bellowed in frustration, "Where the fuck am I going to go?! I'm in a goddamn cave, for crying out loud!"

"Doesn't matter. You're staying in my lap, where I can hold you."

"This is ridiculous!"

"I agree." He grabbed her chin. "Look at me."

Nyra ignored him, rubbing her face with the pads of her fingers, her skin itching as she tried to reign in her anger. A low, vicious sound had her sliding her gaze to the giant warrior beneath her.

"Did you just fucking growl at me?"

"Why do you have to make everything so difficult, woman!?" He cupped the globes of her ass, squeezing handfuls of it as Nyra tried to ignore the instant surge of heat to her core. "Had there been more time, I would have spanked your ass for disobeying me again. But seeing as the Sun is almost up, it'll have to wait. There are more pressing matters that need to be discussed."

"What is it with you and the Sun?" she poked him. "Are you going to turn to stone when the first rays of light hit you?"

"No, actually," he chuckled, arching a brow as he massaged her flesh. "I will turn into a dragon. A very large, *silver* dragon." His smoky voice swarmed around them, the underlying meaning in it hovering in the air like a silent threat.

Nyra went still as his words slowly settled in. "What are you saying?"

"You asked me for my name." He searched her face. "It's Raiden."

They stared at each other in silence, shock and awareness hitting her when realization finally dawned. She jumped back, scrambling to get away, but before she had a chance to do so, two strong hands grabbed her, pulling Nyra flush against an expansive chest as she twisted and kicked.

"Stop fighting me, for fuck's sake!" Raiden's arms locked around her again, caging her arms against her body. "How many times do I have to repeat myself? I'm not going to hurt you!"

"H–How is this possible? You're–" she choked on air, eyes wide. "You're human. I–I thought...But the Captain said–"

"I told you already, I'm a Raijin. We are dragon shifters, we can choose to take both mortal and beastly forms."

"I know what it means, but–but how are you *alive*?" She gaped at him, disbelief taking over her initial fright. "All those history books–they're filled with the violent butchering of the Raijin until every last one of them was completely wiped from the face of the earth. How did you survive?"

Callused fingers caressed her face, Nyra's heart growing from the subtle sign of affection.

"They're wrong," Raiden said. "Not a single Raijin was ever killed. We've been–" he searched for the correct word, "cleverly *hiding* in plain sight."

"What?" Taken aback, Nyra could only stare at this undeniable proof of a living legend. "But so many books, they all speak of thousands of years of aggression against your kind. How have you managed to stay hidden for so long?" She froze as a new realization slithered in. "Are there more of you?"

He searched her gaze, taking his time before he answered, "Yes. But it's not so simple, Nyra. There is a certain curse that affects us. It's as much of a blessing as it is a hindrance."

"I don't understand." Everything was unfolding so fast. "What curse?"

Streams of yellow light played across Raiden's striking form.

"Shit. There's no more time." Lifting her off, his fingers wrapped around her wrist, pulling Nyra along as they ran for the spot where she had initially woken up.

Spinning around, he grabbed her face, staring long and deep into her eyes. "Listen to me. I'm ancient. Older than you can even imagine. Time has taken away my ability to shift between my two forms at free will, and because of the curse of the Raijin, I am forced to stay in my dragon form until the next Full Moon, until eventually I am no longer able to do so altogether, thus becoming a Kaminari." Sunlight cascaded across the ground, reaching for them like greedy fingers of eerie ghosts. "Do not be afraid of me. Even in my dragon form, it is still me, Raiden, the man. The one that you've spent the entire night with. No matter what happens, you are safe with me. I swear to you, I will never let any harm come to you."

The Captain's last words to Nyra resonated in her head.

She had to know.

"Were you hunting for me? After that fire in the village?"

"Yes." Pain laced his features as Raiden struggled to stand.

"Why? Did you want to punish me for the attempt on your life?"

Strong arms wrapped around her. "Sweet girl, it seems your hearing is impaired today. I was searching for you because you are my fated mate."

Relief washed over her. *He was never going to kill me. The Captain lied.* "What does that mean exactly?"

Fingers cupped the back of her head, fisting her hair. "It means that you are my other half, the one chosen for me by the gods themselves. The only one that can tame the beast within me." Angling her head, his nose trailed up her throat, licking and sucking on the skin as he went along. "You're mine to protect," *–lick–* "to cherish," *–lick–* "to fuck and to love," groaning when she shuddered against him.

Feelings of shame returned as Nyra remembered how Raiden had rejected her in the pool. *Maybe there's something wrong with me.*

"Yes," he grumbled, dragging his tongue over her jaw, "you're still talking."

His mouth crashed down, taking away her ability to form words, erasing all doubts as his greedy hands explored her body. Tongue sweeping across hers, licking, sucking, grinding in the most primal way.

"You're magnificent, Nyra. And if we had more time I would spend it all between your thighs, worshiping you like the beautiful creature that you are." A cascade of emotions played in his stormy eyes, claiming her mouth one last time before pulling away. "Are you ready, little vixen?"

"For what?" she said, breathless from their kiss, swaying slightly on her feet.

"To meet the silver beast."

Was she? She swallowed. "Yes."

"That's my brave girl. My good little mate." He pointed to a spot behind her. "Stand there, and remember. You're mine. I'm giving you until the next Full Moon to come to terms with it. Once that time is up, I will be coming for what belongs to me."

"And what's that?"

He grinned. "Your heart."

Before Nyra could wrap her head around his words, a beam of brilliant light filled the cave, forcing her to lift her arms to shield herself.

"Look at me," the deep, booming voice ordered, her heart thrashing like a caged animal. It was like the clash of a thousand drums.

Ever so slowly, Nyra lowered her shaking limbs.

And gasped.

Piercing eyes of the most striking blue color stared back at her over a colossal snout with rows upon rows of razor sharp teeth, the rest of the creature's mammoth form coming into view as it shifted on its four legs.

"Holy shit."

Massive wings with a never-ending sea of shimmering silver scales covered its impressive body, its long tail whipping back and forth like a lethal flail as it deftly circled Nyra. Smoke billowed out of its flaring nostrils, its ears twitching.

The dragon stepped up to her, lowering its giant head.

"Climb on, little prey," Raiden rumbled. "It's time we went hunting."

CHAPTER

9

Soaring through the clear blue skies with his female on his back, Raiden's heart swelled with pride. And not only because he had found his fated mate.

It seemed as if Nyra hadn't been that shocked when he had revealed his identity to her, as if somewhere deep down, her subconsciousness had already recognized the obvious signs that were right there in front of her all along.

No two Raijin were ever alike. There was only one silver dragon with his scale markings in existence. Only one with pale blue flames of fire. His mortal form resembled his beastly one, both in temperament and physical characteristics, making him intimidating and lethal even as a human. And his little vixen had accepted him and their bond without much hesitation.

A small mercy in their otherwise tumultuous world.

"What's that?" Nyra's sweet voice reached him, her slender hand pointing to a spot in the distance.

"It's best if we talk through our minds, pretty girl. We wouldn't want to cause a riot down there."

Silence stretched between them, only the soft swooshing of the wind filling the space.

"How long have you been able to hear my thoughts?"

If dragons could grin, Raiden's sharp fangs would surely be making an appearance right now. *"Since the beginning. It's how I recognized you for what you are to me in the burning village."*

"So everything that I ever thought of in the cave—"

"Yes."

"—and before that, in the forest—"

"*Yes, Nyra.*"

"*Fucker.*" She gasped. "*Oh God, that means that in the tavern, you–*"

A burst of fire escaped him as he full on roared with amusement. "*I heard it all, wildling. How you find me impossibly handsome, and how my scent entices you, and how you can't wait to feel my cock inside of you, molding your pretty little pussy as I–*"

"Alright! I get it!" she yelled out loud, her voice getting lost in the wind. "This is so fucking embarrassing."

"*No need to be ashamed. It pleases me that my mate finds me so irresistible.*"

"*I'm never going to hear the end of this.*"

Movement below caught Raiden's eye. It appeared almost as if– "*It seems that good fortune follows you, wildling. Hold on tight.*"

He dipped, plunging at a recklessly sharp angle, so steep that any other human would have been screaming from fear. But not Nyra. Shouts of joy mixed with loud bursts of laughter followed them as she clutched on to his thick neck, her thighs gripping his muscles like two bars of steel as they plummeted towards the ground.

It was just another undeniable confirmation how this glorious being was made just for him.

Dark blue waters of the Endless Sea stretched as far and wide as the eye could see, the land of the Kingdom of Sota now only a miniscule smudge on the horizon. A massive pod of thirty humpback whales floated on its crystal surface, their enormous bodies languidly gliding along as an eerie melody swept through the air.

"Amazing!" Nyra breathed, astounded. "I've never seen so many whales in one place before!"

"That's because it's very rare that they travel in such large numbers. They're moving to warmer waters for the season, which means that there are at least a couple of future mothers among them."

"What is that sound? It's hauntingly beautiful."

"It's the song of the humpback. It's their way of communicating amongst each other. The males are known to sing to impress the females during mating season, sometimes even to ward off other potential suitors."

She leaned down, fingers stretching towards the nearest whale, Nyra's entire body splayed across his back. *"How are they not scared of you?"*

"They have no reason to fear me, little prey," he purred with contentment at the contact. *"They feel my calmness, which is why they're allowing us so close. Besides, I may be a predator but I do not attack just for*

the sake of it. I kill to feed and to defend myself when provoked."

"Are you saying you've never killed an innocent before?"

"I have, most certainly. But not intentionally, Nyra. Many innocents die daily as an unfortunate casualty of famine and war. Sometimes we, the dragons, are the indirect cause of death and suffering, other times it is a necessary evil to keep the balance of the universe. I am merely another link in the chain of life."

"What about that village, the one that you burned down to the ground before I shot you? Why did you kill all those people? Was that also a necessary evil?"

Raiden's thoughts wandered to that day, one of his life's biggest regrets perhaps. "Your Captain tricked me. His soldiers attacked me and then hid amongst the villagers. I couldn't tell them apart..."

Nyra's heart ached for him. She knew all too well what regret felt like. "Why would he do that, though?"

"It's a long story." The winds picked up, the air cooling. "We should get back. Night is fast approaching and I don't want you freezing to death."

"Yes, master," she teased him. "I am at your mercy, after all."

Groaning, Raiden prayed to the heavens for patience, and for the iron will needed to endure until the next Full Moon.

❖

Time passed, days turning to weeks as Raiden took Nyra out flying until she felt at ease with the vast expanse of the skies and the absence of land below. When they weren't soaring, he was teaching her. About his kind and the world around them, about man's history and the shaping of their universe.

She absorbed it all, soaking up the priceless knowledge until she could recite it out loud in her sleep, until she started correcting him when Raiden purposefully made a mistake, just so that he could watch her blossom from pride.

He had quickly realized how her confidence was frail, as much as Nyra loved to pretend otherwise. He had a feeling that her life as a dragon slayer and the uncertainty of her future still clung on to her, that a part of her still doubted Raiden and his intentions. Whether or not she would end up burned to ashes or her head tied to a chopping block.

Like hell he would let either of those options come to fruition. No one threatened his little mate. Not even the fucking king of this kingdom. And today, Raiden would show her just how serious he was about protecting her.

"Where are we going?" Nyra's curiosity always got the better of her. Not an instance had passed when she hadn't asked him the exact same question.

"We're going to Akira."

"You can't be serious. They'll shoot us both as soon as they spot us!"

"They can try, wildling, but they won't accomplish anything. As you know, I can't die unless you administer the killing blow, and they'd have to get through me to get to you."

"This is insane," she said. *"Why are we going to the capital?"*

"We're visiting a certain someone."

"Who?"

"Patience, pretty girl. You'll see soon enough, we're almost there."

Sure enough, the red stone towers of the royal palace came into view, their nine spires soaring towards the sky as Raiden skillfully avoided them.

Screams rang out from the humans, their cries of terror filling the air as Raiden landed on the palace's vast terrace, prowling towards the open double doors with a very tense Nyra on his back. His tail whipping back and forth, scattering any potential idiots that would dare to attack them.

"What is the meaning of this?!" a gruff voice met them as Raiden filled the massive Royal Reception Room, his body so large that his heavy tail remained on the terrace.

Shifting, his gaze landed on the source of his irritation. A middle aged warrior stood in front of the throne where the king sat, with rich brown curls and a ragged scar across his nose, his cobalt blue military garments adorning a strong masculine body. His face stern as he glared at Nyra, whose heart pounded so erratically that Raiden could feel the thundering beats against his scales.

"Do you know this man?"

"That–" she answered. *"That's the Captain of the King's Guard. The one that I told you about."*

He snarled. *"The very same one that threatened you?"*

"Yes."

"Excellent." He inched closer.

"Raiden," Nyra's nerves bled through his thoughts as he prowled forward. *"What–what are you doing?"*

"Teaching him a lesson."

"You can't hurt him."

"Why ever the fuck not?"

"He was only doing his job. Please."

Groaning in disappointment, Raiden said, *"We'll see how he behaves first."*

"Dragon slayer!" the Captain's voice echoed around them. "I see you have failed to fulfill your mission, yet again. You know what the punishment is in this case." His lips curled wickedly. "I hope you've said your goodbyes to Margot. It's a pity she'll also die because of you."

"Do not speak to her, filthy maggot!" Raiden roared, baring his fangs as his tail slithered into the room. "Do not even look in her direction if you value your life. Get on your fucking knees and beg for mercy, for she is the only reason why you are still breathing, mortal!" His tail struck out, snapping in the air.

A wave of panic washed over the male, his eyes wide with fear as he looked back and forth between Nyra and the silver beast in front of him.

Snarling, Raiden's tail snapped again, hitting the robust Captain, sending him flying across the air. "Either you're deaf or very fucking stupid." His tail smacked him, "I believe it's the latter," over and over again, playing with the measly human like a cat would play with a mouse. "*Beg.*"

"Please," the Captain whimpered, blood staining his neck where an ugly gash could be seen.

"I can't fucking hear you."

"Please!" He cried out, trying to crawl away, only to be pressed into the ground by Raiden's massive paw, the Captain's head thrown back in agony as he screamed for mercy.

"I will color these walls with your blood, rat, before I turn everyone in this precious palace to dust." His jaw snapped, saliva dripping from his lethal fangs as he stalked towards the wounded male.

"Raiden!" the king suddenly bellowed, throwing himself forward, kneeling with his face planted on the ground, his body shaking as all color drained from his face. "Have mercy on us! We are your humble servants. Whatever it is that you desire, it is yours! Riches, maidens, land –"

"Do not insult me, old man," Raiden rumbled. "I do not need your petty bribes. You will wipe Nyra Haldane's records clean, granting her a royal pardon, never to be evoked by any of your successors. That is the price for the lives of you and your worthless servants."

"Done!" the king shouted, shaking uncontrollably as he crawled towards Raiden, kissing his scales in holy devotion. "Thank you! Thank you, oh great one, we are eternally obliged to you! We honor you and your wisdom–"

Flicking his paw, the king scurried backwards.

"Satisfied, little prey?"

"Yes, take me home." She paused, as if thinking. *"By the way, you never told me. When is the next Full Moon?"*

"Why? Do you mean to thoroughly violate me?"

She smirked. *"Maybe I wish to thank you."*

"I'd much rather be ravished."

She smacked him, a full on belly laugh erupting from him as Raiden ran from the Reception Room, ignoring the still rambling king. Soaring towards the slowly darkening sky, the faint outline of the Full Moon peeking through.

He had a mate to claim.

CHAPTER

10

"Come here, wildling."

She swallowed, her throat dry as Nyra glided through the pool toward Raiden, her body painfully aware of every stroke of water against her naked flesh.

Strong hands gripped her waist, dragging her forward. As if by reflex, Nyra's arms went around his neck, legs wrapping around his middle, molding herself to Raiden's powerful human body. Her stiff nipples pressed against his solid chest. His hard cock snug in between, poking Nyra's abdomen as his velvety shaft rubbed on her clit.

"You're exquisite," he murmured, hands gliding across her skin, exploring every one of her dips and hollows. His eyes hooded, hungrily roaming over every visible inch of her skin. "So fucking soft," he praised, yanking her head back, sucking on her throat. Dragging his tongue over her jaw and across her lips.

Her mouth parted, welcoming him, tongues licking each other. Moaning when he slipped a thick finger into her core from behind, pumping languidly before he added two more, as she ground against his steel shaft. Her swollen clit throbbing, pussy weeping.

"I should threaten more men if this is how you'll be thanking me."

"Oh, gods," she rasped as Raiden curled his digits, rocking her hips. "How long do we have before you turn back into a dragon again?"

He chuckled, licking the inside of her mouth. "That depends."

"On what—oh, fuck." Breathless, her pussy contracted as more slick coated his fingers.

"On whether or not you accept me as your mate."

Gripping his hair, she bit his lip. "Do I have a choice?"

"You always have a choice, Nyra," he groaned, squeezing her ass with his free hand.

"What happens if I don't accept the bond?"

"I'll turn back into a dragon and remain one until the next Full Moon. Nothing has to change."

She stilled. "But you've waited so long."

"And I can wait some more, pretty girl." His wrist turned, fingers curling inside of Nyra. "I'll never force you to do anything that you're not comfortable with."

Her heart clenched, his sincerity making her realize that he meant every word. Would it be so horrible to be tied to him? To wake up and go to sleep beside this beautiful male? To spend her days learning and flying through the skies without a single care in the world, completely free for the first time in so many years, the very same freedom that Raiden had so selflessly gifted her. A man that has shown her more affection and devotion than any other person in Nyra's entire life.

Realization struck her. There had never really been any doubt in her mind, she would have done anything to stay by his side. Even begged him to keep her.

"Raiden," she said, locking her arms around his neck, "make me yours."

He froze, his fingers slipping out of Nyra. "What did you just say?"

Their lips touched, six little words whispering against them, "I accept you as my mate."

Mouth crushing hers, Raiden lifted Nyra out of the water, his massive hands cupping the globes of her ass as he carried her over to the large bed that she had been sleeping on since coming to his lair.

Licking her neck, he lowered them onto the bed. "Do you remember what I promised you in the forest, wildling?" Parting her legs, he lined himself up with her entrance. "It's time I kept it." His cock thrust in, filling her up to the brim.

She cried out, arching her back from the fullness, her legs wrapping around Raiden as he began to move.

"I'm going to fuck you nice and slow until you beg me for more." He rocked his hips, his arms braced beside her head, pulling out all the way before plunging back in, over and over until she started moaning without pause.

"Oh, gods!"

He growled, biting Nyra's throat as he leaned down. "I'm getting tired of you calling out someone else's name while I'm inside of you, little prey." His tongue swirled around her tight nipple as he thrust faster, harder. "Who am I?"

"Ah, fuck–Raiden–"

Thrust. "Louder."

"Raiden!"

He bit down, sucking on her pearly buds as he increased his pace. "You're mine," *–thrust–* "only mine." *–thrust–* "My woman." *–lick–* "My companion." *–suck–* "My mate." *–thrust, thrust, thrust–* "I'll take such good care of you," *–lick, suck–* "whatever you need. I'll provide for you."

"More." She clawed at him, fingers digging into his back. "Please, I need more!" a loud moan erupted from Nyra, her pussy creaming at the glorious feel of his thick cock.

"Only if you say the words."

Scratching at him as Raiden pistoned in and out of her, she bared her neck to him, her cunt stretched to the limit as she began to clamp up. "I claim you as my mate."

His teeth sunk in, jaw locking around her throat just as she exploded. Endless cords of hot cum shot into her at the same time, filling her until her tight canal couldn't take anymore, until his milk was dripping out of Nyra around his thick shaft.

"And I claim you," he murmured softly, peppering kisses along her jaw, "as my fated mate." He flipped her around, his cock still lodged inside of Nyra. Lowering himself onto her drenched body, he suddenly pulled out, only the tip filling her entrance. "Better make sure my seed is nice and deep in there." Then shoved back in. "Hold on tight. It's going to be a long night, wildling."

EPILOGUE

Six months later

Flying through the clear blue sky, Nyra's arms spread out beside her, her thoughts wandered back to the beginning of her journey. To the very same one that had forever changed her life.

"Do you have any regrets, wildling?"

"Never," she answered, heart growing from the sound of her mate's voice in her mind. From the feel of his silver scales beneath her as they soared over the Endless Sea.

"I wish to show you something."

She smiled. He *always* wished to show her something, as if her delight at witnessing the many splendid things that he'd come to see during his long existence brought him joy, as well.

Landing on a remote island, she jumped off his powerful back, scanning her surroundings. "What is this place?"

Countless rows of the tallest trees that Nyra had ever seen in her life reached towards the sky, their crowns overflowing with various exotic fruits, while waves the size of entire palaces crashed into rocky cliff sides.

A firm hand rested on her shoulder, Raiden's smoky voice vibrating against the shell of her, "This is the Isle of Ur Chisisi. Home to a very dear friend of mine, wildling."

"Who is he?"

"Who said it was a he?"

She frowned. "You never told me about any of your female companions. I'm not sure I want to meet her."

Chuckling, his muscular arms wound around her, pulling Nyra back against his chest. "Don't worry, little vixen, it's nothing like that," his voice trailed off, gazing somewhere far off in the distance. "She helped me when I was wounded. It was a long time ago, she might not even remember me."

Their fingers linked together as they began to walk towards the tall trees. "Oh, so she's old. Well, why didn't you say so? Now I *truly* have nothing to worry about."

Head thrown back, Raiden roared with laughter. "I never said she was old, either. Not in the usual sense of the word, anyway."

"What!?" she smacked him across the arm. "Is she pretty?"

His nose scrunched up. "I suppose, I haven't really paid that much attention to her physical appearance."

"What do you mean? What's wrong with her?"

"Nothing, wildling, except that she could probably level me with the ground if I ever were to get on her nerves."

Confused, Nyra said, "What do you mean?"

"Let's just say that she's the commander of a very powerful immortal army. I was too busy admiring her warring skills to notice anything else."

"Don't be so humble. You're one of the most powerful dragon shifters alive."

"I am, little mate, but she has something that I never will. The blood of the gods."

The first line of trees passed them by, the melodic tune of the birds welcoming them as the two of them went deeper into the forest.

Raiden leaned in, murmuring in Nyra's ear, "Let's talk about something more interesting. Like what I'm going to do to you once I get you back in my bed. How I'm going to feast on your pretty little–"

She kissed him, swallowing his words before they could form on his lips. "Then let's get this over with already."

The End

(For now.)

ACKNOWLEDGMENTS

A big thank you to each and every one of you that keep coming back and reading my stories. I am eternally grateful for you and the trust that you put in me every time that you open one of my books.

To the publisher and the group of wonderful and very talented authors that are also a part of this series, it has been an absolute pleasure working with you!

To my proofreader and friend, Kara: thank you for your infinite patience and willingness to put up with my crazy schedule (and for being so damn fast!).

My team: I cannot thank you enough for everything that you've done for promoting my work! You are all rock stars!

ABOUT THE AUTHOR

Isabella Khalidi is an International Bestselling and Amazon Top 10 author. She lives in a small town in Europe where she spends most of her days writing and nights dreaming up new magical worlds. *To Claim a Silver Curse* is her seventh novel and the prequel to her upcoming epic dark fantasy romance series *Legends of Kaminari.*

For more news and the latest information visit her site www.isabellakhalidi.com and don't forget to sign up for her newsletter. You can also follow her on Instagram @isabellakhalidiauthor.

OTHER WORKS
BY ISABELLA KHALIDI:

1. *The Forgotten Kingdom Chronicles (in reading order):*

The Snows of Nissa:

https://www.amazon.com/gp/product/B0BZQ75MW1

The Storms of Fury:

https://www.amazon.com/gp/product/B0C199S14T

The Sands of Titans:

https://www.amazon.com/dp/B0C19B1FPK

The Plains of Wrath:

https://www.amazon.com/gp/product/B0C198SRTL

The Valley of Tears:

https://www.amazon.com/gp/product/B0CT57WDPJ

2. *Bound by Flame:*

To Claim A Silver Curse by Isabella Khalidi:

https://www.amazon.com/dp/B0CLKWDQLF

WORKS BY ISABELLA KHALIDI WRITING AS BELLA DURAND (MONSTER ROMANCE):

Roses for the Damned

https://www.amazon.com/dp/B0CJ39DSHP

Lilies for the Cursed

https://www.amazon.com/dp/B0CLD9QTJJ

OTHER TITLES IN THE BOUND BY FLAME SERIES:

To Keep An Emerald Rose by Elayna R. Gallea:

https://www.amazon.com/gp/product/B0CMPTCJ2X

To Ignite A Pyrite Spirit by Callie Pey:

https://www.amazon.com/gp/product/B0CLL16M2G

To Snatch A Gilded Laurel by Alex Callan & Angelica Babineaux:

https://www.amazon.com/gp/product/B0CLL2SMH1

To Spare An Opal Soul by River Bennet:

https://www.amazon.com/gp/product/B0CN89DJQN

To Scorch A Quartz Thorn by Fleur Devillainy:

https://www.amazon.com/gp/product/B0CLKZBT3W

To Hunt A Ruby Remedy by Jen Lynning:
https://www.amazon.com/gp/product/B0CLKZ8DKL

To Web An Obsidian Villain by Vasilisa Drake:
https://www.amazon.com/gp/product/B0CN49VBVP

To Embrace An Onyx Heart by Sirena Knighton:
https://www.amazon.com/gp/product/B0CLKVVF23

Printed in Great Britain
by Amazon

51560058R00081